Heartbreak Café

6

JUST DESSERTS

ellfie
BOOKS

www.ellfiebooks.com

An Ellfie Book

First published in America by Fawcett Books, New York in 1989
First published in Great Britain by Armada in 1989
Reprinted in Great Britain by Diamond books in 1994
This paperback edition published in 2021 by Ellfie Books
An Imprint of Ellingstar Media

alloyentertainment

Published by arrangement with Rights People, London

A CIP Catalogue record for this book is available from the British Library

Paperback ISBN: 978-1-9164482-6-1
Mobi eBook ISBN: 978-1-9164482-7-8
ePub eBook ISBN: 978-1-9164482-8-5

Typeset by M Rules

EM
ELLINGSTAR
MEDIA

Ellfie Books.
Ellingstar Media Ltd.
37 Warren Street, London W1T 6AD
www.Ellingstar.com

www.HeartbreakCafe.LA

Janet Quin-Harkin

Janet Quin-Harkin is better known these days as *New York Times* bestselling author Rhys Bowen, writer of the historical *Molly Murphy* and *Royal Spyness* mystery series. She has won the Agatha Best Novel Award and was nominated for the Edgar Best Novel. In the eighties, when this series was written, she was dubbed by one newspaper as "the Queen of Teen Romance." Janet/Rhys is a transplanted Brit who now divides her time between California and Arizona. You can visit her website at www.rhysbowen.com

JUST DESSERTS

Chapter One

Ever notice how time doesn't pass evenly? It always either speeds up or stands still just when you don't want it to. If you're sitting in the dentist's chair or in the middle of an exam you haven't studied for, an hour can go on for ever and ever. But if the cutest boy in the universe asks you to dance, it seems like the band stops playing almost as soon as you've hit the floor. And time certainly seemed to speed up that summer at the Heartbreak Cafe. Just when I was having the most fun time of my life!

In the past, summer vacations had seemed to go on forever. By the middle of August I was always bored to tears with sitting by a pool and would even begin looking forward to going back to school. This summer was different, though. I wished it would never end. Not that I thought waitressing was the greatest job in the world, but having my best friend and my boyfriend working alongside me made the hours fly by. There was always something happening, too. With our crew of regulars, hardly a day went by without something just a little weird going on! Howard would get a new idea for a science fiction movie, or Ashley would discover a new diet that let you eat all the chocolate you wanted, or Art would find a new way to con his friends into buying him a meal. All these things made life fun, and I came to work every day wondering what would happen next. It was a shock, therefore, to realize that summer was almost over and that soon my life would not be centered around the Heartbreak, but around school.

It had been a pretty uneventful day at the Heartbreak.

Hardly any regulars had come in. Just the beach crowd was there, and they ordered their hamburgers, ate them, and left. Joe and I had worked the early shift and actually planned to get off work at the same time and go to a movie, something that hardly ever happened since we started dating. At around one o'clock Joe went to stretch his legs for a moment. He didn't come back for a while and, of course, just then everyone and his brother came up from the beach at the same time, demanding hamburgers.

I was rushing in and out of the kitchen with loaded trays, flipping hamburgers as I passed and rescuing baskets of french fries before they got cremated when Joe strolled in again, grinning to himself.

"At last!" I said, shoving a loaded tray into his hands. "Table four!"

He delivered it, then came back into the kitchen.

"You were out for a long time," I said.

"No I wasn't! I just walked round the block," he said, then added playfully, "Maybe it seemed like a long time because you always miss me so much when I'm away!"

"Hah!" I said. "I missed you because there was nobody to help cook the hamburgers."

He came up very close to me. I could feel his warmth, and it made me a little dizzy as always. "Come on, admit it, Deb," he said. "The time you spend without me beside you is cold and grey. I bring sunshine to your drab little life."

"Your ego grows from minute to minute," I said. "We'll have to enlarge the doors around here pretty soon."

He ran a finger down the center of my face, over my nose and lips. "Go on, admit it's true," he said.

"Not at all," I said, trying to keep my face frozen in a calm smile even though his fingers on my lips made my knees weak. "You have no effect on me whatsoever."

"Not even when I do this," he asked, leaning down just enough to brush his lips along my neck.

"Joe!" I warned, jumping back. "Not here. Everyone can see us!"

"They're all busy with their hamburgers," he said, laughing.

"You are as incorrigible as ever," I said, laughing as I fought him off.

"I know that word," he said. "It means cute and sexy, right?"

"You know very well what it means. Don't try that dumb act with me. I've known you long enough to realize that you're pretty darn smart."

"Oh, I know that," he said. "I'm just not too wild about words with twenty-nine syllables." He walked away, looking around the kitchen. "But I do know what incinerated means," he added, looking meaningfully into the french fryer.

"Oh, no," I wailed, springing over to the fryer and lifting out a basket of little charred strips.

"What am I going to do with you?" he said, trying to sound serious. "I can't even leave you for a minute. I thought I'd trained you well enough that I could trust you to cook french fries by now."

"It was your fault," I snapped, hating to be criticized even in fun. "You distracted me."

"You just told me I had no effect on you whatsoever," he said. "In which case you should have smelled the fries burning."

I held up a handful of wet lettuce and glared at him, and he backed away. "No, don't you dare throw that at me," he warned. "You'll only have to wash more."

"It would be worth it," I said. "One of these days, Joe Garbarini . . . !"

He chuckled to himself as he put in more fries. This was just a normal morning for Joe and me. His grandfather, old Mr Garbarini, always complained about our fights. Why couldn't we sing and write poetry and give flowers like boys and girls when he was young? he always asked. The reason was that we enjoyed fighting much more. It kept us both on our toes.

"I guess you must be getting very old and doddery if it takes you half an hour to walk around the block," I commented, having thought up my next batch of insults.

"Actually, I got distracted," he said, and a big grin spread across his face. "I ran into something that was definitely worth looking at."

"Bikinis on the beach, no doubt."

"Much more interesting than that."

"A new motorcycle?"

"Even better," he said, and the grin spread. "Big stuff going on down on Beach Row again."

"Not again!" I said with a sigh. Beach Row was just behind

the cafe. It was an up-market street of little boutiques and trendy cafes whose owners never failed to let us know what they thought of having a noisy teen hangout in their area. "They've had something going on there almost every day this summer."

Joe nodded in agreement. "Today's different. There's something really big going on, Deb," he said.

"What do you mean, 'big'?" I asked.

He looked around in case someone else might be in the kitchen. "For one thing, I heard a rumour that Paradise Inns is supposed to be looking for a site in this area."

"They want to build a Paradise Inn in Rockley Beach?" I asked in horror. "Where would they fit a whole big resort complex around here?"

"Give you three guesses," he said.

"Here?"

"Right behind Beach Row is the only flat piece of land in the area, right?" he asked.

I shook my head, unworried. "It's okay. They can do whatever they like, your grandfather would never sell – would he?"

Joe was unworried, too. "Nah," he said. "It would take more than a giant international corporation to scare my grandfather into doing anything he didn't want to do." Ain't that the truth

"Then everything's all right?" I asked.

Joe sort of nodded and shrugged at the same time.

"So what else was going on? You didn't spend all that time watching rumours fly."

"Oh, that," Joe said. "Some dress designer is holding an outdoor fashion show at La Lanterna."

"I didn't realize you were into fashion," I quipped.

"This kind of fashion I am," he said, giving me a knowing look. "It was, er, different."

"I'll have to go look. I want to make sure I'm dressed right when I go back to school this autumn."

He laughed. "You wouldn't want to go back to school looking like that, Deb," he said.

"How do you know?" I asked. "May I remind you that back in the days before I came to work here, I was known as a fashion plate."

"Now you're known as a hamburger plate," he said, grinning.

"Most amusing," I said, giving him my most withering stare.

"Anyway, I can guarantee you wouldn't want to look like those models," Joe said with assurance. Obviously my stares no longer had any effect on him except to make him grin.

"Do you think I can't afford top-class clothes anymore, or is it that my taste has slipped since I started mixing with people like you?" I asked, trying to sound indignant.

"Fine, then," he said. "If you want to start dressing like that, I'm not going to be the one to stop you."

There was something about the way he grinned that made me suspicious.

"Exactly what were they modeling?" I asked.

"Leather minis with bikini tops," he said smoothly. "Little tiny leather bikini tops. And the most interesting new swimwear . . ."

"Oh," I said. "No wonder you took such a long break."

"I did not! I came right back, right after the girl with the miles of legs and—" He slipped on his uniform jacket and raised his eyebrows up and down when he turned back to me.

"I'm going to go see for myself," I said firmly. "It's almost time for my break anyway."

"Maybe you can find something to wear to your senior prom," he called after me as I went out through the back door. I was halfway across the dusty area behind the cafe, the not-so-glamorous part of Rockley Beach where the fishermen's huts were, when I heard someone calling my name from a dilapidated doorway. I looked up and saw Howard's glasses glinting in the sunlight.

"Psst, Debbie. Over here," he whispered, beckoning to me.

I came closer and he emerged from the deep shadow. His hair was spiked as if he'd put his fingers in an electric socket, and he was wearing his same thick glasses and a revolting purple and orange T-shirt. "What's wrong, Howard?" I asked. "Why are you hiding in someone's doorway?"

He looked around. "I want to surprise everyone," he said. "Is the cafe full?"

"Pretty full," I said.

"Who's there? Art?"

"I think Art has just come in," I said. "And Brett and Josh, too. No Ashley yet."

"She wasn't in yesterday, either," Howard commented. "I hope nothing's wrong with her."

"Howard, she doesn't have to live here, you know," I said, although she practically did. So did Howard.

"Rats," he said. "I really wanted Ashley to be in on this."

"In on what?" I asked.

He came closer and put his face a few inches from mine in that unnerving way he had, then gulped a few times. "My latest invention," he said. "I'm going to unveil it this afternoon."

"What is it?" I asked suspiciously. Howard lived for science fiction. He had already disrupted a movie being shot nearby by creating an octopus and a shark, and his brain was constantly buzzing with ideas on how aliens could take over the world in every gross way possible.

"Okay," he said, gulping nervously again. "It's behind this building. Do you think now is a good time to bring it out?"

"Sure, I guess so," I said hesitantly. Howard didn't need too much encouragement.

He took my hand and dragged me into an alleyway behind the expensive shops on Beach Row.

"Look," he said. "What do you think of it?"

He pointed and I found myself staring at a pretty realistic-looking dragon. It was about as big as a dog. "Wow, Howard," I said, "that's really impressive. Is it for a movie or something?"

He gulped again excitedly. "No, it's for the cafe," he said.

"The cafe? Does it carry hamburgers on its back?"

He giggled. "No, nothing like that. For promotion! You know how those stores on Beach Row are always promoting themselves these days and are always rude about us? Well, just wait until everyone sees this. They'll all want to come and eat at the Heartbreak instead. They'll love us!"

"What exactly do you plan to do?" I asked, not really sure whether to be amused or impressed.

"Send it down Beach Row and lead people to the Heartbreak," he said. "See, I've got the remote control right here. It runs along on those wheels, and it breathes very realistic-looking fire. When it lifts its wings, you see it has Heartbreak Cafe written on the underside of them!"

"Very ingenious," I said, "but don't you think you should try it out in the car park first?"

"Oh, I've tried it at home," he said. "It works great! And think what a splash it'd make on Beach Row this afternoon. All those photographers!"

"I don't know, Howard . . ." I began.

"Trust me," he said. "This will really make them sit up and take note of the Heartbreak!"

Before I could say another word, he flipped a switch. The dragon came to life and took off down the alley towards Beach Row. I did have to admit it was very impressive. It sped along, its wheels invisible under its large claws, its wings going up and down, and smoke coming out of its mouth. It reached Beach Row and Howard turned it into the street. We could hear the oohs and aahhs as we came round the corner after it.

"It's going a little fast, Howard," I said. "Don't let it get away."

"Don't worry," he said, breathlessly. "I'm in complete control."

Just as he said that, the dragon hit a parking meter and swerved off to the right, straight for La Lanterna and the fashion show.

"Howard!" I yelled. "Stop it before—"

Too late. Howard wiggled his switches desperately, but the dragon kept on going. We could hear screams and the crash of breaking china. We pushed forward to see some women standing on their chairs and the dragon, now with a tablecloth draped over it, chasing the announcer. Half-covered in a white cloth, with spaghetti sauce stains dripping down the side, it no longer looked like a toy dragon at all. Instead it seemed like something out of one of the horror movies Howard liked watching. It was clear the patrons of the fashion show were alarmed, to say the least. Right through the middle of the fashion show the dragon continued, forcing a girl in a leather miniskirt to do a very impressive vault over the railing. The manager had climbed up on a table and was clutching one of the customers. Howard's dragon continued until it reached the edge of the platform, where it stopped for a moment, puffing fiery smoke up into the sky, then toppled down on to the sand of the beach below, landing with an impressive crash.

Howard and I exchanged a nervous grin.

"I guess it works just fine," he said. "It made them sit up and take notice of us, didn't it?"

"You can say that again," I said, looking at the chaos at La Lanterna.

"Do you think I should go and pick it up?" he asked. "I don't want it to get sand in the machinery."

"If I were you, Howard," I said, "I'd wait until things have cooled down a little here."

"Good idea," he agreed.

I took his arm and we walked quickly back to the cafe.

"So?" Joe called out to me when Howard and I came in, "see anything unusual?"

I looked at Howard. "Unusual? No, nothing at all really. Did you see anything unusual, Howard?"

He shook his head. "No, nothing at all."

Chapter Two

Like I said, it had been a pretty ordinary day at the Heartbreak. When we told Joe about the dragon, he laughed a lot at first.

"I just hope Howard hasn't got the Heartbreak into any trouble," I said. "They're not too fond of us down on Beach Row as it is."

"Who's going to link a dragon with the Heartbreak?" Joe asked, still grinning.

"Unfortunately, it had our name painted on the underside of both wings," I said. "It was supposed to be an advertisement."

"Do you think they'll believe us if we tell them we knew nothing about it and it was the work of our resident maniac?" Joe asked hopefully.

"Frankly, no."

"I didn't think so," he said. He looked up. "Uh-oh, here they come now," I followed his gaze to the car park, where two angry-looking men, plus a police officer, were on their way towards the cafe.

"You kids have gone too far this time!" the men yelled as we came out to meet them. Joe tried to tell them it was an accident – an advertising stunt that went wrong – but they just didn't want to listen. It's never very pleasant when adults yell at you, and by the time they left both Joe and I were exhausted.

"You don't think they can really close the cafe, do you?" I asked.

He shook his head firmly. "There's nothing they can do to get rid of us. We meet health codes, we've got off-street parking, and we've been around longer than they have. So what can they do?"

"They seemed to hint that we wouldn't be around much longer, that they'd figured out a way to get rid of us," I said.

"That was just talk," he said. "They want to get the Paradise Inn people to build here, that's all. But if they try anything they'll find out that nobody pushes the Gabarini family around!"

His confidence reassured me, and we were laughing about the dragon incident before Joe left. I let him get away a few minutes before four because he had a delivery to make for his parents, and I waited for Pam and Mr Garbarini to take over the evening shift. Pam arrived right on schedule.

"Hi, Debbie," she called happily as she came in through the kitchen door. "Anything exciting happen today?"

"Nothing special," I said not looking up from the burgers I was cooking. "Howard built a mechanical dragon that breathed smoke and it got loose at a fashion show on Beach Row—"

"He did what?" she shrieked.

"It was very impressive," I said. "He was trying to advertise the Heartbreak in a unique way."

"I swear, one of these days that boy is going to blow up the world," she said. "Was there any trouble about it?"

"Not much," I said. "We had a policeman and a couple of

shop owners in here complaining that we were bad news and that they were going to get the cafe closed down."

"That's terrible," she said. "Sometimes I think someone should be assigned as Howard's permanent bodyguard. He's dangerous."

"He meant well," I said. "He thought we needed some publicity to compete with the places on Beach Row."

"He certainly got some for you, didn't he?" Pam said, looking half worried, half amused – just the way I always felt when I thought about Howard. "They can't really get the cafe closed, can they?" she asked.

I shook my head. "Joe says the Heartbreak meets all the codes. We tried to tell those men that the dragon was an accident, but they're not very pro-Heartbreak these days. And to make matters worse, Joe heard that the company that runs Paradise Inns is thinking of putting a resort in the area. Those Beach Row snobs would love it if the company bought the cafe site and put up their resort right here."

"I sure hope they don't do that," she said.

"Me, too. Joe says his grandfather would never sell, so I guess we don't have to worry."

"So how was the dragon?" Pam asked a moment later.

I grinneed. "It was great. The way it flapped its wings and turned its head as the fake fire came out. I wish you'd seen it."

"I don't suppose I'll get a chance now, huh?"

I shook my head. "I don't think so. It crash-landed on the beach, and nobody's dared to go near it since."

"Oh, well," Pam said then, "I had some exciting news too, but after that, it sounds kind of tame."

"What happened?" I said.

Pam took her uniform from its hanger and shoved her purse into the cupboard. "I just saw the first signs of autumn today!"

"The leaves are turning gold already?" I asked, peeking out through the back window to inspect the trees beyond the car park. They were still leafy and green, just as they had been all summer.

"No!" Pam answered impatiently. "The sales have started for next term – file paper and lunch boxes! Terrific prices, too. I couldn't resist. I started stocking up for the year. Do you think ten packets of file paper will see me through my senior year?"

I looked over at her. Pam was usually so calm, so steady. She had a round, friendly face and moved slowly and gracefully most of the time. But today her face was flushed and excited, and she seemed ... well, almost emotional.

"Pamela" I said with a big grin, "you must be the only person in the world who could get excited about file paper! A clothes sale I could understand, but file paper! You can't wait to get back to school, can you?"

"Well," Pam said, sounding defensive, "it is our senior year and there will be lots of fun things to look forward to. We'll be on the committee of clubs and apply to colleges and walk around looking at freshmen as if they were worms ..." She paused and peered at me curiously. "Don't tell me you're not excited about being a senior? We've talked and dreamed about it since we were in junior high."

I gave a sigh. "Somehow it's different," I said. "It's just no big deal anymore. Maybe it's because everything's changed so much in my life this year. I used to have time to be in the plays and clubs, and I always took it for granted that I'd go to a good college ..."

"You still will," Pam said. "You're clever."

"Clever but poor," I said, turning away abruptly. "Gee, look how much lettuce we've gone through today," I babbled so I wouldn't have to discuss something as scary as my future. "I'd better cut up some more right away or Mr Garbarini will be furious when he comes in."

Pam came over to me and perched on a stool behind me. "There are such things as scholarships, Debbie," she said. "They're for kids like you – so you can go to a good college."

"Kids like you, not me," I said. "You'll be offered tons of scholarships. Every college in the country will fight over you. As for me ... well, I'm okay. I'll get into college, but they won't want me badly enough to offer me a scholarship. Especially since I won't have the time for extra studying or activities this year."

"You're going to keep on working at the cafe once school starts?" Pam asked.

"If I don't it will be community college or nothing," I said, "and I really don't want to go to community college. Imagine going to college with your *mother.*"

Pam smiled at my horrified look. "Your mom's going back this autumn?" she asked. "Good for her!"

"She's planning to get her bachelor's at least," I said. "The way she was talking last spring, she might even go for her master's and be in college forever. Can you imagine having your mother spying on you every time you talked to a boy?"

Pam grinned. "I can imagine Joe spying on you every time

you talked to a boy," she said. "Won't he be going there too this autumn?"

"He's going to try going part time," I said. "I thought for a while that he was going to put off college for now, but I'm glad he didn't. You know how hard it would be to get back to studying later. That's what my mother found. Now at least he agrees it's a good idea to get all the general education courses out of the way. Then he can transfer later."

"He wants to transfer to a four-year school? Good for him," Pam said.

"Of course he does," I said proudly. "Joe might act as if education doesn't mean much to him, but it's only an act. He really wants to go to college, but I think he's afraid he won't be able to handle it with the cafe to run. Of course, you know Joe – he'd never say he's scared of not doing well."

Pam nodded. "He'll do fine at Shoreline," she said. "Is he looking forward to it?"

"I guess so," I said. "He's not thrilled about community college. It's not the same as going away, living in a dorm, all that stuff. That's why I have to save every penny I can this year – so I won't have to go to Shoreline, too."

"I admire you," Pam said. "I know I couldn't handle a job and studying, too."

"That's because you spend sixteen hours a night at the library," I said. "I don't fall apart if I don't get straight As anymore. I think working in the cafe has altered my priorities a little. What bugs me more is that I won't be able to be in the play or in any clubs. I hope I can at least find the time for the tennis team – that is if I'm still good enough . . ." My voice drifted off as I realized that this was the first year I hadn't practiced at the country club all summer. I'd been there a few times as someone's guest, but that wasn't the same. How awful if I didn't even make the team this year. Maybe it was good that I was working at the cafe. I could always use that as an excuse.

I went on cutting lettuce feverishly, trying to fight back the sinking feeling that always overtook me when I thought about how much everything had changed and how uncertain the future was. It was funny to think that this time last year I'd still been living in the big house on the golf course, I'd still had a successful lawyer for a father, and I'd fully expected to be captain of the tennis team and go straight to some Ivy League school! What a difference one little divorce makes!

"It's four o'clock, Debbie," Pam said, taking the knife out of my hand, "Time to go. Aren't you going to a movie with Joe tonight?"

"We sure are," I said. "A miracle has finally happened – you and Mr Garbarini are running the cafe, and Joe and I can actually go on an honest-to-goodness date!"

Pam laughed. "You guys don't need dates anymore," she said. "You act more like an old married couple every day!"

"We do not," I said, trying to look shocked and horrified. "I'll have you know that Joe is a perfect gentleman."

Pam giggled. "I didn't mean like that," she said. "I meant that you're with each other so much that you've slipped into a routine together."

"That's certainly true," I said. "It's really neat to feel that you know somebody well enough that you don't have to watch what you are saying or put on an act with them."

Pam's face took on a wistful, dreamy expression. "I keep hoping someday that will happen to me," she said. "Maybe when I get to college."

"Of course it will happen to you," I said. I glanced at the car park. "Uh-oh, here's Mr Garbarini!" I watched the old man struggle to get out of his battered old pick-up truck. "I'd better get out of here before he finds something I haven't done!"

"How does he look?" Pam asked nervously.

"Fine. I think he's finally recovered completely from his heart attack, don't you?"

"He certainly has," she agreed. "But I meant, does he look as if he's in a good mood?"

"Who knows?" I said. "With Mr Garbarini you never know when he's going to explode."

"I know," she said, peering over my shoulder as the old man slammed the truck door, looking around with his perpetual scowl, and began to shuffle towards the building. "He still scares me."

"He's a big pussycat underneath," I said. "Just stand up to him, that's what he likes. You know these Garbarini men, it's all bluff and show."

"You should know," Pam said. "You seem to have his grandson wrapped around your little finger."

"Only because I do twenty push-ups a morning to keep in shape," I said as I headed for the cloakroom to change out of my uniform.

"I thought you said he was the perfect gentleman," Pam reminded me with a quizzical look.

"That doesn't mean he's always happy about it," I said, grinning. "He still keeps hoping . . ."

After I'd changed I grabbed my purse and was about to rush out of the front door just as Mr Garbarini came in the back door.

I was a second too late. "Hey, there, DebbieLeslie, where are you off to in such a hurry?" Mr Garbarini called after me. He always ran my first and last names together and made it sound like some exotic pasta dish.

Obediently I came back. "I was just on my way home," I said.

He sighed, an exaggerated sigh. "Young people these days, they have no pride in their work. They skip out the moment their shift is over. So where's my grandson?"

"I said he could go early," I said. Big mistake. Mr Garbarini scowled.

"*You* said?" he bellowed. "So you're in charge around here now, are you? I'm glad to know that. A few months here and you've taken over."

"I didn't mean it like that," I explained. "Joe had to make a delivery for his parents so I said I could cope until you and Pam got here. You see we have a date tonight – we're actually going to a movie together – and Joe didn't want to be late."

"Ah!" the old man said, relaxing his scowl. "Finally you behave like the young sweethearts! That's better. A date! Does that mean no more fighting in my cafe?"

"I can't promise that," I said, smiling sweetly. "May I go now? I'm meeting Joe at five."

"Go! Go!" he shouted, waving his arms and shooing me out of the door. "And make sure that no-good grandson of mine buys you flowers!"

"And serenades me outside my window?" I called, winking at Pam as I headed for the door.

"Enjoy your evening," Pam called back. "There'll be a quiz in the morning on the subject matter of the movie!"

I made a face through the serving hatch and ran out to my car. I lowered the top and drove up the canyon from the beach with the wind in my hair. I loved the feeling of freedom I got when I drove with the top down. My little convertible was the one extravagance I had managed to carry over from my life before the divorce. It was to pay for the car's upkeep that I had originally taken the job at the Heartbreak. Maybe I'd also wanted to pay back my parents for putting me through all that stuff. I knew it would be the sort of place my mother disapproved of – rowdy and loud, with cheap hamburgers and motorcycles parked outside. I had never intended to keep working there, but the cafe just grew on me. I began to really like the regular customers who had seemed so weird at first. They were still weird, I guess, but I liked them anyway. I also began to care about the owner's grandson, which was something else I swore I'd never do.

I smiled to myself as I swung the little car round the bends. Joe was so much a part of my life now, it was hard to remember that we had started off hating each other. *I hope nothing changes when school starts again,* I thought. *I hope I can still fit in working down at the cafe with everything else.*

Reaching the top of the canyon, I turned on to the highway, past the new shopping centre. It said GIANT BACK TO SCHOOL SALE in big letters on the board in the car park. I frowned at the sign. School used to be the most important thing in my life. I used to love going back to school every autumn, to be with my friends and take part in all the activities. I was still looking forward to it in a way. My stomach even turned a happy little somersault when I thought of all the things that were waiting for me in my senior year. It would be fun to dress up in togas for Homecoming week, to have a senior prom and graduation, and to eat lunch in the senior quad, only ... only I didn't want this summer to come to an end. I had a horrible feeling that once school started again, once Joe enrolled in college, nothing at the Heartbreak would ever be the same!

Chapter Three

I turned off the highway and passed the pseudo-Spanish gateway that marked the entrance to the condos where I now lived with my mother. A wrought-iron sign outside proclaimed, *The Oaks, a Planned Community for Today's Family.* Inside there were plain old condos, each with a rock and a juniper bush outside, plus a pseudo-Spanish arch over the front door. I'd moved there with my mother after my parents sold our big house and split the proceeds to live on. My father had gone to write screenplays at an artist's community down the coast, and we got the condo. As you can probably tell, it was still not our favourite place in the world. After a big house with lots of space and a huge back yard, it was still a shock to have a bedroom the size of a cupboard and to hear every fight next door through the paper-thin walls. Thank heavens I had the Heartbreak and didn't have to spend much time at home. I would have gone nuts trying to endure a summer beside the pool with all those kids splashing and yelling.

I put the car in the garage and noticed that my mother's little Honda was still there. No newspaper today, obviously. She had got a summer internship at the local daily paper, which had been great experience for somebody who had been Mrs Perfect Housewife for the past seventeen years. I was really proud of the way she had held up after the divorce. It couldn't have been any easier for her than it was for me, and yet she had thrown herself instantly into the process of making a new life. I guess we were both stronger now than we were a few months ago.

"How come you're home?" I asked, coming in and throwing down my purse on the sofa. "Is it a holiday in the newspaper business?"

Mom looked up from the kitchen counter, where she was sitting, glasses perched on the end of her nose, studying something.

"Oh, hi, honey," she said. "I've got the college catalogue here."

I opened the freezer and took out the ice cream.

"Any fun courses?" I asked, spooning a giant scoop of Cookies and Cream into my bowl.

"Make one for me while you're at it, will you?" Mom said. "I feel like ice cream today. I need something to sweeten me up."

"You?" I spluttered. My mother had been a total health food nut for years. We got tofu in our salads and organic everything when my mother cooked.

"I just feel like having some ice cream today," she said. "Ice cream is a comforting sort of thing."

I put a generous scoop into a dish and handed it to her, then perched myself on the next stool. "Is something wrong?" I asked. "Did something bad happen at the paper? Is that why you're home so early?"

"No," she said quietly, then paused to take a mouthful of ice cream. "The paper's over. Today was the last day of the internship."

"Oh, that's too bad," I said. "Still, you knew it was just for the summer, didn't you?"

"Of course," she said. She took another spoonful of ice cream.

"They asked me to stay on, Debbie," she said. "To go on their full time staff."

"That's great, Mom," I said. "I always knew you were good. Will you be able to fit it in with your college course load?"

"No way," she said, laughing. "I'd have to drop out of college."

"Drop out of college?" I yelled, almost dropping my ice cream spoon.

"Debbie," she began, "just hold on a minute. Before you get all upset—"

I cut her off. "Mom, listen to me, you cannot drop out of college! I won't let you!"

"Why not?" she asked. Her eyes were amused as she looked at me.

"It's obvious, isn't it? You went to college to finish your degree. You dropped out once to marry Dad. You can't wimp out again."

"I wouldn't be wimping out," she said. "I'd merely be moving into the business world."

"As what?" I demanded. "Did they offer you a reporter's job?"

"Not exactly," she said. "The position is as a general researcher. But it could lead to reporter."

"So what you're saying is that you're giving up college to be a gofer?"

"Not exactly," she said, flushing. "And I think you're being very rude, Debbie."

"Sorry," I said. "I didn't mean to be rude. I just don't want to see you make a giant mistake."

She toyed with the catalogue. "I'm just beginning to question the validity of college, that's all. I mean, look at all these courses – philosophy, Greek culture, beginning Chinese … what do they have to do with real life?"

"They get you a degree, which means qualification, Mom," I said. "Remember when you went for those interviews and everyone turned you down because you didn't have the right piece of paper? What if the reporter's job doesn't work out. Where will you be then?"

"But I'm tired, Debbie," she said with a sigh. "I'm sure college seems like the greatest thing in the world to you, and it should. But I'm not eighteen anymore. I saw my advisor this afternoon – she wants me to take biology this quarter to fulfill my science requirement."

"So? Biology wasn't so bad," I said.

"You know how I hate creepy crawly things," she said. "When I took high school biology I fell off my stool."

"How come?"

"We were dissecting this worm, and I thought it moved and was coming towards me."

I started to laugh. She saw my face and laughed too. "It was a very big worm," she said. "I hit my elbow, and everyone laughed. I never liked biology after that."

"Mom, all you do is get yourself a nice lab partner to do all the dissecting for you," I said. "That's what I did. And I've got all my old notes. I'll help you."

She reached over and patted my hand. "Thanks, honey," she said. "I know you mean well and I know that maybe I'm wrong to 'wimp out', as you put it, but I have a job offer right now and something inside me tells me I'd be crazy to turn it down."

"Well, I think you're crazy not to finish your education," I said. "I won't have you dropping out of college, young woman, and that's final!"

I had only intended my speech to make her laugh, a sort of parent-child reversal act, but her face flushed again. "I seem to remember," she said slowly, "that you don't like it when I try to control your life. And now you think you can control mine."

"Only because I don't want you to make a giant mistake," I said softly. "What if this job turns out to be nothing?"

"It won't," she said. "I'm already well-known at the paper. They like my work."

"I remember Ralph liked your work so much that he used all your research for his project and won an award for it," I reminded her. "Without giving you credit! That could happen again."

She sank back on to her stool and buried her head in her hands. "Oh, I don't know, Debbie," she said. "I just don't know what's best. I've got to earn my living eventually. I'd like to be able to put you through college."

"Don't worry about me," I said. My voice was a little shaky because I did worry about how I'd get through college. It would have been nice to have parents who could support me.

"A parent is supposed to be able to provide for her child," she said sharply.

"I don't notice Dad doing much providing, and he doesn't seem upset about it," I commented.

She scowled. "Maybe that's one of the reasons I'd like to get a job. I don't want to end up like your father – a drop-out and proud of it."

"That'd never happen," I said. "You and I take after Grandma Tregner. We've got staying power." I put my hand on her shoulder. "Promise me you'll think this over carefully," I said. "And that you won't do anything rash without talking it over with your daughter first."

"Okay, Mom," she said.

"Good girl," I said, and we both giggled. "Now, if you'll excuse me," I said, glancing over at the clock on the living room wall, "I have got to go and make myself beautiful. Hot date tonight."

She perked up instantly, just as I thought she would. "A date. With whom?"

I laughed. "Who do you think? Who is the only boy who's been in my life all summer?"

"Oh," she said. "I just thought …"

"I know," I said, grinning at her. "You hoped I was finally getting tired of Joe and had found someone more suitable. Go on, admit it."

"Well," she said hesitantly, "I do have to admit that I'd have preferred someone more, er …"

"Boring?" I asked.

"Suitable," she said. "Where are you going on your date, anyway?"

"El Sleazo Motel," I quipped. "Honestly, Mom, Joe and I are going to a nice PG movie about happy college students … just like I'd hoped you'd be."

She laughed at this. "Oh, go away," she said, still laughing. "And Debbie?"

"Yes Mom?"

"Don't do anything rash without talking it over with your mother first, will you?"

Chapter Four

We came out of the movie into warm night air.

"Good movie, huh?" Joe asked. "I thought it was pretty funny."

"I hope you don't pull any stunts like that when you're at college," I said. "Although I can't imagine wild parties like that going on at Shoreline."

He didn't say anything. We turned towards my car, which was parked on the other side of the street. "Have you picked up your catalogue yet?" I asked. "My mom got hers today."

He took my arm and led me across the street. When we reached the other side he said, "I've changed my mind. I'm not going."

"You're what?" I yelled so loud that some people a few cars away looked up, alarmed.

"I've decided not to go to college," Joe said, shrugging his shoulders as if it was no big thing.

"What are you talking about?" I asked. "Of course you're going to college. I thought you had this all sorted out. You were going to get all your GE requirements out of the way at Shoreline and then transfer to a good college."

He looked uncomfortable. "Yeah, well, maybe I've changed my mind again," he said. "Maybe it just seemed possible then and it doesn't now. Maybe I don't even want to go."

"Don't want to go?" I burst out. "Joe, you've dreamed about getting away, about making a better life ever since I've known you."

"Deb," he said, putting a restraining hand on my arm, "How can I? When would I ever get time to study? I'm not going to do it if I can't do it well."

"We'll make time for you," I said. "Your grandfather can get another waitress. A full-time waitress."

"You know as well as I do that the problem is my grandfather," Joe said angrily. "He won't trust his precious cafe to an outsider. He wants me around all the time."

"Tell him you can't do it anymore because you're going to college," I said.

He shook himself free of me. "You don't understand how families work, do you?" he demanded. "We're Italian – family is everything. Family comes first. I can't let my grandfather down."

"Seems like he's letting you down if he stops you from getting an education," I snapped.

"What would you know about it?" he asked. "Your father walked out on you. Is anyone better off because of that? You don't know a thing about families."

"I know what's important," I said frostily. "You know you're college material and I hate to see you wasting your life."

"I'm not wasting my life," he said. "I might even go to college later, and even if I don't, running a restaurant's not that bad."

I turned to face him angrily. "Joe, you know it and I know it – compared to an education, the Heartbreak Cafe isn't worth a hill of beans. One of the things that attracted me to you was that you were so strong and sure of yourself. Now I'm beginning to think I was wrong about you. As soon as the going gets tough, you chicken out."

"I'm not chickening out," he said in a cold tone. "I'm doing my duty."

"Why can't you admit it? You're scared that college will be very different and you're not sure if you can handle it," I said. "Duty is just a convenient excuse not to even try."

"Fine, if that's what you think," he shouted. "Don't bother to give me a ride home, I can walk from here. I know you wouldn't want to be seen driving with a chicken."

He hurried off in the other direction, leaving me with my mouth open, trying to call after him that I was sorry, that I hadn't meant to upset him at all.

Why do things never work out the way you want them to? I thought as I drove home alone. I was sure I could appeal to Joe's pride to make him change his mind about college. I didn't want to make him mad. It was just that I knew from my friends' older sisters and brothers what happened to kids who put off going to college until later. They never went at all. I didn't want that to happen to Joe.

This had been the evening of the great wimp-out, I decided. I wanted only the best for my mom and for my boyfriend. I didn't want either of them to end up in nothing jobs. So how come they couldn't see that going to college was the only answer?

I brooded about Joe until I fell asleep, one minute lifting the phone to call him, then being scared of what he'd say if I got him on the phone. He was not the type of guy who'd easily forgive or forget being called a chicken. He prided himself on his toughness. I realized now that I had gone way too far, come on much too strong.

As usual I was interfering in other people's lives again, I thought miserably. I just hoped I hadn't driven Joe away forever.

I tried to put myself in his place, to think how it must feel to want to go to college but knowing you couldn't without letting your family down. I still knew so little of what the real world was like. I guess I still expected every parent to want the best for their children, even though my own perfect family had crumbled to nothing recently.

The next morning at work I apologized to Joe as soon as I came in. "I'm really sorry about last night."

He didn't look up. "Aha," he said, acknowledging me.

"I had no right to butt into your life like that."

"You're right," he said stiffly. "You had no right because you can't put yourself in my place, however hard you try."

"I know," I said. "I overreacted and I said things I never should have said to you. I never would have said those things, except I'd already been through the same scene with my mother."

"Your mother's dropping out of college?" he asked, the stiff expression on his face softening for the first time.

"They've asked her to stay on at the newspaper – as a researcher."

"Well it makes sense, doesn't it?" he said. "Why go to college when you've already got a ready-made job?"

"Joe!" I exclaimed, already losing my cool, understanding image, "she had to drop out of college once before. Now she's not that far from her bachelor's degree. It's dumb to throw that away just for a lowly newspaper job."

Joe looked straight at me, his dark eyes serious. "Debbie, did it ever occur to you that not everyone in the world can be a professor or a doctor, or even wants to be? Some people even like lowly jobs. Your mother's a grown woman. Why can't you let her make up her own mind?"

"You're right," I said at last.

"I'm always right," he replied, and gave me his usual wicked grin.

"If you're so clever," I said quickly, "then go to college. Forget about the Heartbreak and just go!"

He came over to me and put his big hands on my shoulders. "You know what?" he asked gently.

"What?" I asked. The feel of his hands on my shoulders still make any logical thoughts fly from my head.

"You're an interfering, meddling, do-gooding, busybody," he said, "and one of these days, you're going to get what you deserve."

"And what is that?" I asked sweetly, because I could see his eyes were laughing into mine now.

"Someone who can shut you up," he said, and kissed me right on the lips.

Chapter Five

I was glad that Joe and I were back on good terms again, although sometimes I sensed that he hadn't quite forgiven me, or that maybe I had wounded him more deeply than I intended. Maybe I was being ultrasensitive, but he seemed aloof and brooding sometimes, staring dreamily out the window while he worked. I guess it can't just have been me, because his grandfather noticed it too.

"So how come you two don't fight anymore?" he asked. "All afternoon you are polite to each other! A miracle."

"We're just behaving like two mature adults," Joe said, giving me a wink.

Mr Garbarini threw up his hands in aggravation. "Mama Mia, wonders never cease," he said. "My grandson is finally growing up! Does that mean I can finally trust my cafe to him? I can finally take some time off? Play bocce ball with Giovanni and checkers with my friends, like any man is entitled to at my age?"

Joe gave me a quick nervous glance. "You see," the glance said. "How can I go to college when my grandfather needs more time to himself?"

I could tell it weighed heavily on his mind. There were times when he even slipped out alone on breaks, returning with a worried look on his face. I tried not to mention college again and just hoped that we could return to our old teasing but loving relationship.

Fortunately we had other things to think about at the Heartbreak. It seemed as if we were constantly in trouble with our neighbours in the up-market stores. We had managed to coexist peacefully with them before, but now it began to seem as if they were picking on every little thing we did. If one of the cafe regulars parked an old surfing buggy outside one of the boutiques, the owners were instantly hammering on our door, demanding that it be moved. Our music was suddenly too loud, although it was no louder than it had always been. If kids sat outside on the steps on a Saturday night talking and laughing, someone called the police, even though people sat outside talking and laughing at the fancy bars and nobody called the police on them.

At first we couldn't think what we had done to make everyone so angry with us. Howard went around in deep gloom, convinced that it was his dragon that had made everyone so upset. Then one day we had a visit from the owner of Secret Hang-ups, a very trendy clothing store on the corner beside us. A group of kids with motorcycles were at the cafe and he came to complain that they were using his parking spaces.

It was rather funny in a way. He was a shortish man with bright ginger hair and lots of freckles, and he obviously thought he was being very brave to face all of us big, bad teens.

"I just can't allow you kids to park your motorcycles in my parking area," he said, waving his arms around as if he were doing the breast stroke. "I mean, they look so . . . angry, don't they. And think of my customers."

"Okay, okay," Joe said. "They were just leaving anyway. There's no harm done, so let's just forget about it."

"But there was harm done," the man said, still waving his arms. "They parked in front of my store. Who knows how many customers I might have lost."

He spoke loudly and the whole cafe burst out laughing. He turned to face them, his pink cheeks even pinker now. "You kids think you're so funny, don't you? Well let me tell you, you are not at all popular around here."

"No kidding?" came a voice from the back.

"So, you don't own the beach," someone else shouted.

The man flushed an even deeper red. "You just wait," he said. "If the developers decide Rockley Beach is the right place for the new Paradise Inn, you'll all have to go to another beach, won't you?"

The kids looked at each other in confusion. This information was clearly news to most of them.

"The Paradise Inn people want to build here?" one of the boys asked.

"They're considering it," the man said. "And you know where the ideal site would be, don't you. The only flat area big enough to put a hotel on?"

The kids looked at one another as this sank in.

"Mr Garbarini would never sell, even if Paradise Inns wanted to buy," a voice from the back growled.

The man drew himself up to his full height of about five feet five. "If a giant international corporation like Paradise

Inns wants something, they usually get it," he said. "All we are praying for now is that your nasty loud cafe doesn't give them the impression that the whole area is noisy and full of young punks. They only put Paradise Inns in very select areas, you know."

"So let them choose a select area," one of the kids shouted. "We don't want them here."

"You may not be around long enough to care," the man said, already heading for the door, obviously sensing the mood was turning ugly. "If they want this site, they'll get it, believe me."

The moment he left the cafe erupted into angry noise. Everybody bombarded Joe with questions. Did his grandfather own the land? Was there a way they could get the cafe shut down? Everybody finally calmed down a little when they found that Mr Garbarini had opened the cafe long before any of those snobby shops were there, and the only way they could close the Heartbreak would be if he decided to sell.

Soon, however, the whole of Rockley Beach was buzzing with rumours about the new resort hotel. Some of the kids thought it might be kind of fun to have a great big hotel with a swimming pool in town, but most of us liked things the way they were. There were already enough snobs in Rockley, was the general opinion!

Soon we began to see strangers in the neighbourhood – men in dark business suits who prowled around clutching clipboards, followed by men in jeans who measured things. They even started measuring on the lot behind the Heartbreak, which made the surfers at the back table really mad.

"You can measure back there all you want," Brett shouted out of the window, "but you can tell your bosses they'll have to build their fancy hotel around us."

The man looked up and grinned at us as if we were a cageful of monkeys in a zoo, then carried on measuring.

"What if they do build the hotel next to us?" Art asked, looking at me worriedly. "Imagine a high rise right next to us. It would take away all our sun. Are they allowed to do that?"

"I don't know what they're allowed to do," I said.

"I thought you were the one who liked to go around saving the world," Art said to me. "Can't you do something about this?"

"I wouldn't know where to start," I said. "Besides, I'm sure they're considering a lot of places. Maybe they'll decide that Rockley is unsuitable for some reason."

"Hey, maybe we should help them make up their minds," Brett yelled, grinning at his buddies. He looked around. "Yo, Howard, we're going to need you. Can you build a few things that explode or smell bad?"

Howard jumped up excitedly. "No problem," he said. "What kind of explosion did you have in mind?"

I stepped in right there. "Come on, you guys," I said, putting a restraining hand on Howard's shoulder. "Whoa, Howard, down boy, cool it." I pressed him back into his seat. "Let's think about this for a moment. What they want right now is a reason to get rid of us. And as long as Mr Garbarini owns the land, they can't, can they ? But if they can prove that the cafe is a nuisance or a danger, or even worse, a health hazard, maybe they can make us close down. We have to stay cool. I know that's what Joe would say."

"Where is Joe, anyway?" someone asked.

"He's out somewhere," I said vaguely. Joe had disappeared a few times recently without telling me where he was going. I pushed back all the uneasy thoughts that had been nagging at the back of my head, thoughts I'd tried to ignore. Joe might have a perfectly good reason for wandering out without telling me, but the very fact that he was now deliberately seeking to get away from me, to shut me out, gave me a sinking feeling in my stomach – the sort of feeling you get in a horror movie when you know there has to be something terrible round the corner. Not that I thought he was meeting another girl down on the beach or anything. It was just that I'd thought we'd reached a stage where we told each other everything, and now I realized that wasn't so.

"And where's Ashley," Howard said. "She hasn't been in for a week. I hope she's not sick or something."

"Maybe she's on vacation," I suggested.

"I don't think so," Howard said. "You know what her family's like – not exactly big hearted. They wouldn't want her on vacation with them. Besides, if she was going away, she'd have told us."

"Yeah, have you ever known Ashley to keep quiet about anything?" Art said, grinning at his friends. "If she was going on vacation, she'd have burst in, waving her arms and squealing, 'Hey everybody, guess what?'"

"Hey, speak of the devil!" Josh said, giving Art a dig in the side. "Look, here she is now!"

Ashley burst through the front door, looking as wild and disarrayed as ever. Her long black hair covered half her face so that she had to look up at us through a curtain. She was wearing her usual tight slinky clothes – the shortest miniskirt in the world topped with a bright pink halter. "Hey everybody, guess what?" she called. The group broke into instant laughter, and Ashley flushed scarlet. "What did I do?" she cried, confused.

I went over to her. "It's okay, Ashley," I said. "They weren't laughing at you. It was just that we were wondering where you were and right at that moment you burst in."

Ashley grinned self-consciously. "Gee, it's nice to know you guys were talking about me."

"We were worried," I said. "Howard was scared you were sick."

"Oh no," Ashley said, brushing back her hair with her hand. "I was just, er, busy for a few days. I didn't have time to come down here."

"No kidding?" Howard asked. It was hard to believe that Ashley was ever too busy to come down to the Heartbreak. "Have you got a job?"

"No, I just had . . . things to do," she said. "I only came down because I had to speak to Debbie."

"Oh, sure," I said, flattered that Ashley would have come in just to ask my advice on anything. "Let me just take care of these guys and I'll come and talk. Joe should be back from his break any minute now."

"I just saw Joe outside talking to some guy," Ashley said.

"Oh, where?"

"At one of the old cottages," she said. "They're tearing it down. Which reminds me," she added, her face growing all excited again. "I almost forgot what I wanted to tell you. You got me so flustered and all."

"Okay, Ash, tell us," Art said, slipping an arm round her shoulder. "And while you're at it, why don't you and I share a double root-beer float?"

"You're still lifeguarding, you buy your own root-beer floats," she said, slipping out from under his arm.

"Or better yet, you buy one for Ashley," Howard added. "She's treated you enough times."

"Yeah, but I'm going to be nice enough to listen to her," Art said. "That deserves some reward."

"For heaven's sake, let her tell her news or she'll burst," Brett commented dryly. "Look at her face – she's about to explode."

"I am not," she said, trying to look dignified. "I just hate fighting, that's all. I get enough fighting at home, thank you. Now, do you guys want to hear my news? It concerns you too, you know."

"Okay, go ahead," said Art, putting on a phony interested expression.

"Cut it out," Ashley said, giving him a playful slap. "It's not even funny news."

"Well?"

"There's a man in our car park," Ashley said. "Right behind the cafe."

"Oh, no! A man – wowee!" said Brett. Several other boys broke into noisy comments.

"Shut up, you guys," Ashley said. "This is serious. Why's he there?"

"Maybe he's trying to cross our car park to get to the beach?"

"But he's measuring," Ashley said. "He's got one of those funny surveyor's instruments, and he's got it directed right at the cafe."

"Those men are all over the place right now," Howard told her. "They're trying to choose a site for the new resort hotel."

"Not here!" Ashley shrieked. "They're not going to tear down the cafe, are they?"

"They can't," I reassured her. "Mr Garbarini owns the land so we're safe. They can measure all they want."

"Oh, that's good," Ashley said, beaming at me, "because I don't know what I'd do if the Heartbreak wasn't here. I'd have nowhere to go."

"I know how you feel, Ash," Howard said.

"I haven't been down here for a whole week," Ashley went on, "and I feel as if I've been away from home too long. You guys are really special to me."

Art and his buddies launched straight into a routine about how special they were, and Ashley looked bewildered, just as she always did when she was being teased.

"Come on, Ashley, come and talk to me while I take care of orders," I said. "You can sit on a stool at the serving hatch while I'm working. Then Joe can't say I'm goofing off when he comes back."

She came over and sat down on the other side of the open hatch.

"So what did you want to talk to me about?" I asked. "Some kind of problem?"

"I need your help, Debbie," she said.

I looked up. "Okay."

"I want you to help transform me."

"Into what?" I asked suspiciously. In the past couple of months Ashley had decided she was Cleopatra and then later an alien. "Don't tell me you've now discovered that you're really a leprechaun or an elf?"

She giggled. "That's silly," she said. "There aren't any such things." She leaned over confidentially. "I guess I'd better explain," she said. "You probably wondered where I was all this week."

"Sure. We all missed you."

"I was at Numero Uno," she said.

"Really?" I couldn't hide my surprise. Numero Uno was a cafe over by the country club – a sort of snobby Heartbreak, where rich kids hung out. They served about ten different kinds of espresso and cappuccino.

"You know where I mean?" Ashley asked.

I nodded. "I used to go there a lot when I lived up there."

"Right," she said. "That's where all the kids from that neighbourhood go."

"I wouldn't have thought it was your type of place, though," I said. "Too snobby."

"It's not," she said. "I hated it there. No one even spoke to me."

"So what were you doing there?"

"Looking for a boy."

I couldn't keep from grinning. "Any boy in particular, or did you just decide you needed a rich boyfriend."

"A particular boy," she said, and her face flushed traffic-light red. "I met him down at Jupiter last Friday night. His name's Jason something . . . maybe you know him?"

"He belongs to the country club?"

"He must," she said. "He drove off in a red BMW."

"Jason?" I thought for a moment. "Maybe he moved in after I moved out," I said. "Did he say he was from around here?"

"I didn't ask," Ashley said. "I didn't want to blow it by appearing too pushy."

"And you really liked him?"

"Oh yes. We danced together, and he was so nice, Debbie." Her face became all dreamy and far away.

"But he didn't ask you for your phone number, or say he wanted to see you again?"

"Yes, he asked for my number," she said.

"So he'll call you."

"I didn't give it to him."

"Why not?" Sometimes Ashley was a little hard to understand.

"I saw that car and I knew he had to be rich. I didn't want him to call and get my parents – or worse, find out where I lived – so I said our phone was being repaired at the moment. So he said 'see you around,' but I'm scared he thought I didn't want to see him again, so I've been hanging out all week at all those snobby places. I even tried the pool at the country club, but the lady at the gate was *soooo* horrible. She looked down her nose at me and said, 'This is a members only facility!'"

I giggled at Ashley's imitation. Funny, but I'd never thought about how snobby it was when I lived there. It had just been a place to hang out with my friends. I'd learned so much in the past few months, and I saw that all the places I used to go were stuck up and exclusive. One of the things I liked most about the

Heartbreak was that anybody could come in and if they were friendly, they got along just fine.

"So you haven't seen him since Friday?" I asked.

She shook her head. "Maybe he's been away this week," she said. "I'm going back to Jupiter this Friday night, just in case he's there again."

"Good idea," I said.

"So I need your help, Debbie," she said. "You know, to transform me."

"Into what?"

She leaned over into the kitchen, and I had to pull back the bowl of lettuce before her hair trailed into it. "Into another you," she said.

"Ashley!" I almost laughed out loud. "This guy liked you, not me."

"But he won't like me when he sees where I come from," she said. "Debbie, guys who drive red BMWs don't want to park them outside old crummy buildings like mine with winos asleep on the porch."

"If a person doesn't like you for yourself, he's not worth your time, Ashley," I said. "You should know that."

"Oh, I'll be myself eventually," she said. "I just want to get things going between us. We have to have something in common, right? So I want you to teach me. I want to know what things kids from the country club talk about, how they dress, all that sort of junk." She turned her big dark eyes on me. "You will help me, won't you? This is the first terrific guy I've ever met in my whole life, and he seems to like me, too. I don't want to wreck my one chance because I don't know how to behave."

She leaned so far into the kitchen that she was in danger of toppling into the hamburger I was just making. "Please say you'll help me? Please?"

I sighed. "Okay, I'll try," I said, "although I'm not sure you're doing the right thing, Ashley."

She bounded up from her seat. "Thanks, Debbie, you're a real pal," she said. "You saved my life. Maybe this is really it, the one great moment I've been waiting for. Maybe I've finally met the right guy for me."

It wouldn't have surprised me if she'd burst into song, I thought as I walked over to the sink and happened to glance out of the window. What I saw made me scream out.

"What is it?" Ashley called.

"The man in our car park isn't just measuring anymore," I yelled back. "He's got a bulldozer!"

Chapter Six

The bulldozer was making its way across our car park, heading straight for the cafe. I didn't wait a second longer. Flipping the grill off, I ran out through the front door. Behind me I could hear Ashley screaming, "Get out everyone, they're going to knock down the cafe! We'll all be squashed flat!"

Her statement produced immediate results. I heard chairs being knocked over, a glass shattering, screams and shouts. In fact, it sounded like a poor fight scene from an old Hollywood Western. I barely had time to take in the sounds before I was down the steps and face-to-face with the bulldozer.

I don't think I'd ever realized just how large a bulldozer is before. Now I found myself looking up at the man, perched on that little seat with the huge scooper in front of him. I felt my confidence evaporate rapidly.

"What are you doing?" I shouted above the roar of the engine. "This is private property."

I guess I must have sounded braver than I felt because the driver stopped and leaned down to hear what I was saying.

"You're in the wrong place!" I shouted up at him. "This is private property. It belongs to the cafe here!"

"What?" He cupped his hand around his ear to hear me over the noise of the engine.

"You're making a mistake! You can't bulldoze the cafe!" I

yelled. In midsentence he switched off his engine, and I found myself yelling into silence.

I saw his lips twitch with amusement. I guess I must have looked funny, preparing to stop a bulldozer single-handedly.

"Now hold on a minute here, little lady," he said in a voice with a pleasant southern lilt to it. "I ain't aiming to bulldoze nothing right now."

"Then why are you heading straight for us?" I demanded.

The other kids had surrounded us by now and joined in loudly, "Yeah, you thought you could knock down the cafe first and ask questions afterward. We know how big business works!"

The man raised a big meaty hand. "Whoa, hold on a minute. Hold your horses," he said. "I got my orders, see, and my orders are to leave the dozer here by this fence until it's needed."

"But why would you want to leave it beside our fence?" I asked, puzzled. "Who gave you those orders."

"My foreman," he said. "Beyond that I don't question where they come from."

"But this is still a private car park," I said. "We need all the space for customer's cars."

He smiled pleasantly. "Yeah, but that's for a day or so now, isn't it?" he asked. "When the cafe's closed I can have all the car park I want for my dozer, right? Then we can come in real quick and bulldoze down all these old shacks at the same time."

My brain was hearing but not making sense of what he was saying. I heard someone else in the crowd ask the question for me. "What do you mean, 'When the cafe's closed?'"

"I heard they're planning to sign the papers by the end of the week, then we can move right in and get on with it."

"What are you talking about?" I shouted, wishing that Joe would hurry up and come back. This situation was already more than I could handle. "You've got the wrong place. This is the Heartbreak Cafe. Nobody's going to close it."

"That's not what they told me," he said. "They told me they'd found the ideal site for the new resort right here and that all these old shacks were going to go. They said I was to leave the dozer here until we got the go-ahead."

"I think you'd better move that bulldozer before I call in the police," I insisted. "You can't park it here."

"I'm just following orders, little lady," the man said. "And I got orders to leave the dozer right here, which is what I aim to do." He smiled pleasantly at me again. If he had been closer, I bet he would have patted me on top of my head. "Now, why don't you be good kids and let me get on with what I was doing? You can't do a thing about this cafe now, it's already all decided."

"By whom?" I shouted. "I'll bet nothing's been decided. Mr Garbarini would never sell the cafe without telling us."

"Yeah, he'd never sell the cafe!" Howard seconded. "He wouldn't do that to us, would he?"

"I wish Joe would get here," Ashley wailed. "I don't want them to knock down my Heartbreak."

"I'd better go and call Mr Garbarini," I said hesitantly, feeling the weight of being in charge. "He'll come right down and sort things out."

"I think you'll find everything's in order," the bulldozer man said. "They were talking to the cafe owner yesterday. He was down here with his lawyer."

"Mr Garbarini?" I asked in amazement. "Old man with lots of white hair and big bushy eyebrows?"

"No, a young guy."

"Then they weren't talking to the cafe owner," I said. "I bet one of the store owners from Beach Row was trying to persuade them to force the cafe out of business. That's the sort of creepy thing they would do."

The other kids nodded. "Yeah, they're a bunch of jerks. That's just what they would do," Art said.

"This young guy, what did he look like?" Brett demanded. "Did he have sandy hair?"

"Hey, here comes Joe," Ashley suddenly shrieked. "We're saved!"

All eyes turned down the street to where Joe was strolling toward the cafe, his leather jacket slung over his shoulder as usual.

"Joe, get over here," Art yelled at him.

"Joe, they're trying to close the cafe. Call your grandfather," Howard added.

Before Joe could speak the man in the dozer pointed to him. "That's him," he said. "That's the young guy who was here with the lawyer. He's the one who's selling the cafe to us!"

There was total silence as we all stared at Joe. He shifted his weight from one foot to the other but said nothing. I felt as if I'd been turned to stone. It was Ashley who spoke first: "That's not true, is it, Joe?" she asked. "Say it isn't true. You wouldn't do a thing like this to us."

Joe was looking at the ground. "They offered us a real good price, Ashley," he said. "Far more than this crummy old place is worth. We'd have been fools to turn it down."

Again there was stunned silence. A wall of hostile faces stared back at Joe. I kept expecting him to laugh and break the tension. "Fooled ya, didn't I?" he'd say. "Man, you should have seen your faces."

But he didn't move a muscle. He went on staring out past us as if we didn't exist.

I went over to him and touched his arm, not a hundred percent sure it was really him and not just some body-snatcher from outer space borrowing his body. "Joe?"

He turned to look at me, not blinking.

"Is this for real?"

"Of course it's for real."

"I can't believe it," I said. I could hear the anger mounting in my voice. "How could you? You, of all people. I can't believe you'd let yourself be pressurized into doing something so wrong!"

"Actually," he said, still icily calm, "I went to them and offered them the site."

"You did what?" I cried.

"I offered it to them," he said.

"I . . . don't believe you," I stammered. "You wouldn't do that. Besides, it's not yours to offer."

Joe went on looking at me. "When I told Poppa the figure they were quoting, he didn't need much persuading. He can retire now, comfortably."

"But the cafe, Joe. What's going to happen to the Heartbreak?" I blurted out.

He shrugged, letting his jacket slip down his shoulders until he caught it with one hand. "I seem to remember you were the one who said the Heartbreak wasn't worth a hill of beans," he said.

I sensed those hostile gazes shifting from him to me.

"Hey, wait a minute, don't try to blame this on me," I yelled. "I didn't mean I wanted to see the cafe torn down."

"Oh, no," he said, his voice also rising now. "You're great at starting things, aren't you, but you don't think them through. You told me I was chicken because I wouldn't find a way out of working at the Heartbreak and go to college. Well, now I can go to college if I want. I can tour the country if I want. I'm free for the first time in eighteen years, do you realize that?"

"And what about all of us? What happens to us?" I asked, feeling a lump too big to be swallowed rising in my throat.

"There are other places to go," he said, looking away from me. "Look, I don't feel too great about letting people down, but I had to get out when I could. Sometimes you have to take chances in life, go for things while you've got the opportunity."

I was fighting back tears. "I thought I knew you so well," I said, fighting to keep my voice calm. "Boy, was I ever wrong. The number of times I've boasted to my mother about how you were great at all the things that really matter – like caring about people and honesty and all that stuff! I thought—" I got choked up and fought to get the words out. "I thought you were the best, most uncompromising guy I'd ever met." I began to push my way through the crowd back to the security of the cafe.

"Deb, wait," he called after me. "Don't judge me until you know all the facts. At least listen to my side."

"I don't talk to traitors! In fact, I don't want to talk to or listen to you ever again, Joe Garbarini," I shouted over my shoulder as I fled.

Chapter Seven

The moment Pam showed up for her shift, I grabbed her. "Thank heavens you're here," I said. "I couldn't have lasted another minute."

"What happened?" she asked, concerned.

"Ask Joe," I said, turning to glare at his back. "He'll tell you." Then I ran out of the door and went straight home without saying a word. I was so angry and upset I was sure I'd break down and cry in front of everyone.

Joe called that evening, but I told my mother to say I wasn't at home. She raised an eyebrow and could scarcely hide her delight.

"You two have had a fight, I take it," she asked after she hung up.

"More than a fight," I said grimly. "It's over forever. I don't want anything more to do with that creep."

"I'm so sorry," my mother said, trying to be sympathetic. "And you know, it may hurt now, but believe me, honey, it's for the best in the long run. I could see he wasn't the right person for you."

"I wish I could have seen through him, too," I said. "Then I could have quit working at the cafe before I got so attached to it."

"So you're quitting your job, too?" she asked. Again, I sensed the concealed delight under her calm voice.

"I don't need to," I said.

"Don't tell me that boy actually had the nerve to fire you?" my mother exploded.

"No, Mom," I said wearily. "The cafe's closing. Probably within the week. Dear wonderful Joe turned traitor and sold it to some developers without telling anyone."

She looked surprised, and I realized for the first time that she'd expected Joe's sin to be very different. "That doesn't sound so terrible to me," she said. "In fact, the boy must be smarter than I thought. I wouldn't be surprised if the place wasn't close to being condemned anyway. He was smart to get out while he could."

"How can you say that?" I demanded. "A lot of kids rely on that cafe. To them it's not just a place to come and eat, it's like a substitute family because their own families are so crummy."

"I appreciate that, Deborah," she said, "but these things happen. Joe was just being realistic."

"Joe was being a rat," I said. "What about people like Ashley and Howard? Where will they go now? Where will any of them go down at the beach? They can't pay five dollars for a cappuccino and a croissant at La Lanterna, even if they wanted to go and be treated to snobby stares."

My mother came over and touched my arm. "There's no point in getting upset, honey," she said. "There's nothing you can do about it. The important thing is that now you're free to find yourself a better job. I'll ask around for you at the newspaper if you like."

My stomach did a sharp flip at the thought of finding another job. The truth was that I didn't want to work anywhere else, to start off at square one with a lot of strangers. I'd had to work and fight hard to earn my place at the Heartbreak. Now I belonged. Everyone there was my friend – or at least, that's what I'd thought. I now had one enemy! To push the thought to the back of my mind, I jumped on what my mother had said. "Does that mean that you've decided to take the job at the paper?" I asked.

She smiled nervously. "I thought … that I'd give it a try," she said.

"So you're definitely not going back to college."

"Probably not."

"I see," I said.

She caught my expression and frowned. "Don't look at me like that, Deborah. Maybe college isn't what I wanted after all."

"Or maybe you're scared of flunking biology," I muttered, not quite loud enough for her to hear. It would be better if I said nothing, I decided. I didn't want another person blaming me for their wrong decisions.

"Suit yourself," I said, walking away from her and toward my room.

"So do you want me to find out about a job for you?" she called after me. "I think you'd enjoy it, more than washing-up and waiting on tables anyway."

"I don't know, Mom," I said wearily. "I don't know anything anymore. Nothing makes sense."

She came over to me then and wrapped her arms round me. "It'll work out, honey," she said. "Everything will turn out just fine, you'll see. Maybe we'll both end up as ace reporters on a story together."

I knew she was trying hard to be nice to me, and I tried to say something nice back, but I couldn't. I had a horrible feeling that if I opened my mouth, I might do something dumb like cry. So I gave her my best attempt at a smile before I went into my room.

I really didn't want to face Joe in the morning. *Let him try to cope with the early shift all alone,* I thought as I kicked off my slippers and heard them land with a satisfying thud against the wall. *Why should I ever go back to his crummy cafe? It will be closed by the end of the week anyway, so it doesn't even matter if the customers get poor service and don't come back!*

My whole head was a confused jumble of angry thoughts. I tried to understand what had made Joe behave like such a jerk. I tried to make myself believe that it was really his grandfather who wanted to sell, not him. But every way I tried looking at it, I couldn't forgive him. He'd always claimed to despise people who thought only about money, and yet he'd given in to the first good offer in his life. He'd always claimed to care about people, and yet he'd let down a whole lot of people who counted on the Heartbreak ... I paused as a thought struck me: maybe I was one of those people. I'd felt sorry for Ashley and Howard and the others, but maybe I was really feeling sorry for me. I had been scared and lost after my parents' divorce. I thought I'd never belong anywhere after we left the country club and moved to our condo. And then came the Heartbreak. The first weeks weren't easy and I'd felt like quitting several times a day, but I'd made it. I learned not only how to cook hamburgers, but how to get on with all sorts of kids. To tease and be teased. And then there was Joe. I'd really thought that I'd found the guy I was looking for – a guy I could both trust and love.

I felt that familiar queasy sensation – like an elevator going up too quickly – just thinking about what would happen now. After the Heartbreak closed there would be no familiar faces, no inside jokes, no Ashley or Howard or … Joe. He'd be off somewhere, probably spending his share of the profits from the cafe, and … I'd be back to square one. All alone with no place I belonged.

At least I knew how to cook hamburgers and fries, I thought. I could get a job at any fast-food joint! (Full of strangers who take their food and go, a voice inside me whispered.) I'd find somewhere, just as good, just as fun as the Heartbreak, I told myself breezily. I'd have a blast working there, and when Joe just happened to drop in, I'd pretend I'd forgotten all about him … This brought my daydream to an abrupt halt again. It was actually over – the one and only truly big romance of my life had ended. *How can I be happy without him?* I wondered. *But how can I go on seeing him after what he's done?*

It was with all these confused thoughts in my mind that I drove down to the Heartbreak the next day. I guess I must have looked like a typical snobby teenager as I drove down Rockley Canyon – the top was down on my convertible, my sun-bleached hair was streaming out behind me, and I was playing music loudly on my cassette deck. What anyone watching me wouldn't know was that I was fighting to stay cool. The wind in my face and the loud music were to shut out the panic I was feeling. I knew I had to face Joe, and I had no idea what would happen. Maybe he'd decided he was wrong after all. Maybe he'd apologize and tell me that he'd turned down the developer's offer and we'd all live happily ever after. Right, and maybe pigs might learn to fly! Joe wasn't exactly known for admitting he was wrong and apologizing at the drop of a hat. He was too proud for that – it was one of the things I had liked him for.

I managed to keep up my cool appearance as I strode into the cafe. Joe was already at work filling ketchup and mustard bottles. He looked up quickly when he heard my footsteps.

"I hope you aren't going to throw any more hysterics," he said. "I'm feeling kind of tired."

"What hysterics?" I demanded.

"Yesterday afternoon – screaming and hollering in the car park. That wasn't hysterics?"

I shook my head. "That was just anger. Perfectly reasonable, justifiable anger."

He grinned. "Typical woman," he said. "Screams and rants like a maniac and then says it's reasonable."

"Chauvinist," I growled. "Anyway, you might have considered my feelings."

"And you might have considered mine."

"Yours? Your feelings? In what way?"

"You think I enjoy being humiliated in public, having some girl screeching curses at me in front of half the population of Rockley Beach?"

"Oh, gee, I'm sorry I hurt your precious image," I said. "But I thought you real-estate tycoons were hard as nails. You have to be to ruin other people's lives, don't you?"

He took a deep breath, clearly trying to think of an answer to that and not coming up with one.

"Didn't expect to see you today," he said. "I thought you walked out on me yesterday."

"I didn't walk out on my *job,*" I said. "I made a commitment to work here, and I stay true to my bargains. I'm the sort of person you can count on."

"Yeah, I can see the halo," he said with a sarcastic half-smile. "Saint Debbie always does the right thing." He wiped his hands on his uniform jacket and walked ahead of me into the kitchen. "I'd just like to see what you would have done in my place," he said. "If someone offered you more money than you ever dreamed—"

"I thought you were always the one who made fun of those rich ladies who park their BMWs outside the cafe," I said, following him. "You always said they thought their money could buy anything!"

"It can buy some things," he said, his eyes darting defensively. "Like freedom. Don't tell me you wouldn't have jumped at the chance—"

"At least I would have talked it over with people," I said. "I wouldn't have gone sneaking off alone and made deals behind everyone's back."

"I wasn't free to talk about it," he said. "Poppa didn't want anyone to know until it was finalized."

"I see," I said frostily.

He rolled his eyes. "Oh, I get it, you're mad that I didn't tell you about it in advance?" he said.

"Of course I'm mad," I said. "You might at least have told *me* about it."

"It was none of your business," he said. "It only concerned my family."

"Which shows how important I really am to you."

He sighed and ran his fingers through his thick, dark hair. "Debbie, what has our relationship got to do with a family business deal?"

"Nothing at all, obviously," I said, my voice trembling in spite of my desire to stay cool. "After all, why should you confide in just any old casual acquaintance?" I took a deep breath to calm myself down. "That's just fine," I said. "There are plenty of other jobs out there in the world and plenty of cuter, nicer guys, too."

He came over to me, standing really close, looking down into my eyes. "Deb, so what if we've sold the cafe," he said. "Does that have to affect us? We can still see each other, can't we?"

He put his hands on my shoulders and I moved away, affected, as always, by his closeness. *He's not going to talk me round this time,* I told myself firmly.

"Come on, Deb," he whispered. "Admit it, you came back today because you can't stay away from me."

I shook myself free from his grasp. "Did anyone ever tell you that you have an ego the size of Texas?" I asked.

He grinned, a grin of pure triumph. "I still know how to tease you, don't I?" he asked. "I love it when you get angry."

"Do you take anything in life seriously?" I demanded. "I think this whole thing is another big game for you. You don't care that you've left a lot of people with no place to hang out. You don't even care that you've really hurt me by going behind my back."

"You make it sound as if I was two-timing you or something," he said, also sounding angry now. "Debbie, I didn't sell the cafe to hurt you – or anyone."

"Oh, no?" I turned to stare out of the kitchen window.

It wasn't the greatest of views, just a muddy car park with a couple of weatherbeaten cottages behind it, sheltered by a large tree, but it made my heart ache to realize that it would all be bulldozed into nothingness soon.

Joe came up behind me. "So when this closes, you're just going to walk out of my life?" he asked.

"No, you're going to walk out of mine," I said. "I'll be working at a new job, and you'll be showing off your new sports car and whatever else you've bought with your share of the millions. Our paths won't cross anymore, which I guess is all for the best."

"Debbie," he said, "will you just stop being so angry for a minute? I thought you of all people would understand why I jumped at the chance to get out of this place."

"Oh, I understand," I said sarcastically. "Someone waved a lot of dollar bills under your nose. Money talks, right?"

"Fine, great, if that's what you think," he said. "You don't even want to understand my reasoning."

"All I know is that I thought I knew you so well, and I didn't really know you at all. I'll never be able to trust you again."

"Fine," he said. "In that case, it's a good thing we are splitting up. I wouldn't want a girlfriend who isn't willing to see my side of things. You always were too ready to jump in and judge people. Who decided you were the Supreme Court anyway?"

"Just because I speak out when I see my friends making big mistakes," I said.

"And you've had so much experience of life that you're able to advise them all," he said, matching my sarcasm.

"I know what it's like when the place you think of as home suddenly disappears," I shouted. A picture had come into my mind, one that I had managed not to think about for the past few months. It was a picture of that first morning at the condo, waking up to find my whole world had fallen apart. I hadn't realized until this moment that selling the Heartbreak hurt me so much because it echoed that first, overwhelming betrayal.

I pushed past Joe, grabbing my uniform from the closet. "There's work to be done. I haven't got time to stand around chatting with you," I said, and rushed into the cloakroom to change.

Chapter Eight

I tried to get through my shift as if nothing was wrong, skirting round Joe and making sure I was never in the kitchen at the same time as him – which wasn't too hard because he was doing the same to me. We both had hurt, angry looks on our faces, and I bet if anyone had got us together and told us to stop being so childish, this whole thing might have ended there and then. But nobody did.

And no amount of concentrating on burgers, fries, and shakes could distract me from my problems. Every time I had a moment to relax, I'd wonder why there was a tight band of tension round my head, why my stomach felt as if a horse had kicked it . . . and then I'd remember. Then there was Ashley. I didn't see her come in as I headed across the cafe with a tray piled high. She grabbed my arm. "Hey, Debbie – you and I have to talk," she said.

I must have jumped a mile. The contents of the tray teetered, sending a chocolate milkshake sloshing over into the fries. Before I could stop myself, I turned to glare at her. "Now look what you've done!" I said. "Sometimes I think you should have your head examined. You don't grab somebody when they've got a full tray in their arms."

Her normally wide eyes opened even wider. "Gee, I'm sorry Debbie. I didn't mean to scare you. Here, let me help clean it up."

She grabbed some napkins from the nearest table and started drying off the fries one by one. The hopelessness of her efforts broke the tension and made me laugh. "That's no use, Ashley," I said. "Don't worry. I'll go and get another plateful. Nobody would want to eat chocolate-flavoured french fries!"

A dreamy look spread over Ashley's face. "Chocolate french fries, now there's a thought," she said. Ashley was the world's biggest chocoholic!

"Ashley, how disgusting," I said, but she was beaming.

"Seriously, this is something to work on," she said. "If you make chocolate-flavored french fries, it would be a great way to cut calories. You could even sell it as diet food."

"How?" I asked suspiciously. '

"Well, if you got the chocolate flavour while eating the french fries, you wouldn't need the double chocolate madness afterward, so you'd eat less, right?"

"Hey, can we have our food over here?" a voice growled from a back table. I grinned to Ashley. "We'll talk about it in a minute," I said. "I have got to get this poor guy some new, non-chocolate flavoured french fries."

"Before you go," Ashley called after me, "I have to know if you'll still do it."

The whole cafe looked up with interest. Ashley had a way of putting things that awoke every imagination for miles around. I was embarrassed that everyone was looking at me, and also confused about what she was talking about.

"Do what, Ash?" I asked.

"You know, what you promised," she said in a whisper loud enough to be heard down on the beach.

I'd had so much on my mind that I couldn't remember what I had promised. Did she mean fighting to keep the cafe open? I dumped the plates on the table, rushed back to get a new scoop of fries, and came back to Ashley.

"Now," I said, putting a hand on her shoulder and shoving her down into the nearest seat. "Remind me again what I promised."

She looked hurt. "You know," she said. "You promised to help me."

"Help you?" I was still thinking in terms of stopping bulldozers from crushing the cafe.

"Transform me," she reminded patiently. "You were going to help turn me into a country club person."

"Oh yeah," I said, remembering now. "So you can impress that guy you met."

"You will still do it, won't you?" she asked. "You see, it's even more important than ever now. If they really close this place, I've got to have somewhere to go, and if I finally had a real boyfriend, I could go up to the country club with him, couldn't I?"

"I don't know if you'd have much fun at the country club," I said. "They're pretty snobby up there."

"But I'd be with Jason," she said, beaming again. "Other people wouldn't matter."

"I don't know if this is such a good idea, Ashley," I said.

Her face fell. "But you promised, Debbie," she said. "You can't go back on your promise. I have to know what to say to him. I'm going back to the Jupiter tomorrow night, just in case he's there. It's my only hope, and I was wondering … would you come with me?"

"Don't they always say three's a crowd?" I asked.

"But I'm scared I'll say the wrong thing," she said. "You could be my coach, help me out. I'll watch you and do what you do. That way I won't do anything dumb and look like a fool. You will come, won't you?"

Joe walked across the cafe just then with three plates of hamburgers balanced on his arms.

"Sure, why not?" I said, loud enough for him to hear. "A nightclub sounds like a lot of fun. Who knows, maybe Jason will bring a friend and we can double date. After all, we've both got to find a new place to hang out now that the Heartbreak's closing."

Ashley, naive as ever, didn't realize I was doing any more than talk to her. She smiled from ear to ear. "That's great, Debbie," she said. Her voice was almost drowned out by the sound of plates being banged down loudly on the next table.

I drove over to Ashley's apartment to pick her up the next evening. Frankly I wasn't looking forward to going out one bit. It just added to all the other worries in my life, and the whole plan could very easily go very wrong. Things Ashley planned often did. She had even ended up unknowingly carrying drugs once when she thought she was an alien from another planet. It seemed that every one of her crazy ideas ended in disaster. I tried not to worry as I pulled up outside her building and honked the horn. It was an old brick building in a run-down part of town, and several guys on the street looked up to glare at me as I sat, as out of place as a pearl in a pumpkin patch, in my little white convertible.

As Ashley came down the steps, flustered, gathering

belongings that threatened to slip from her arms, I had my first shock of the evening.

"Do I look right?" she called. "I've been digging through thrift stores all day trying to find the right image."

Ashley was usually known for her tight, sexy outfits – skirts way above the knee, halter tops, skimpy bikinis, fluorescent colours. At this moment she was wearing a silky white blouse, done up to the neck, a pleated skirt, and, although it was a warm summer evening, a blazer with a badge on it. I decided the truth would be less painful in the long run.

"Ashley, what on earth made you dress like that?" I asked as I opened the passenger door for her.

She turned her huge eyes on me. "You don't like it?" she asked.

"You look like the world's youngest secretary," I said, "or a member of a touring Olympic team."

She looked hurt. "But I wanted to look as if I belonged at the country club. Isn't this how rich kids dress?"

"You goob," I said, laughing at the look on her face. "When I lived at the country club, the richest kids paid a fortune to buy clothes that looked as if a hobo had slept in them. The older and more ripped, the better."

"You're not putting me on?" Ashley asked suspiciously. "You're not playing a trick on dumb old Ashley?"

"Cross my heart and hope to die," I said, nodding at the seat beside me. "Get in and we'll call in at my house on the way there. You can wear something of mine if you like."

Her face lit up. "Debbie, you're the best," she said. "I just have to look right for Jason. After all, you could never take a girl for a ride in a BMW if she wasn't wearing the right outfit, could you?"

"Ashley, he liked you last week when he met you dressed as you," I said. "Why do you think he suddenly wants you to look like somebody else?"

Ashley toyed with her long hair. "I don't know," she said. "I just don't want to blow this, Debbie. It's really important to me. He seemed so nice as well as cute. Quiet, clever, more like the sort of guy you'd go for." Her face clouded over. "Debbie, you wouldn't … would you? No, of course you wouldn't. You've got Joe."

"Strike the last part," I said. "I don't think I do have Joe anymore."

"But you're so right for each other," Ashley said.

"I thought so, too," I said, "but I guess I didn't know him as well as I thought. I just can't forgive the way he went behind our backs and let us all down, Ashley."

"Me neither," she said, "but I don't know if I'd be so ready to give up a guy like Joe just because he did one bad thing. Guys like him don't come along too often, do they?"

"I don't know, Ashley," I said, stepping down on the gas pedal so that we roared away from a stoplight. "Right now we're both furious with each other. I'll have to see how I feel when I've cooled down and when I can think about the future calmly again."

We stopped at my condo and exchanged Ashley's Ms Secretary outfit for a pair of long, pleated black shorts and an oversize man's shirt. I also changed her hairstyle, pulling it back into a silver barrette, then gave her just a hint of make-up.

By the time we had finished, she looked quite different – not like Ashley at all. Without the heavy black liner round her eyes and the gobs of mascara, she looked softer and less like an air-head. She stared in the mirror, putting her hand up to her face as if to make sure it was hers.

"Oh, wow," she said. "I look just like you."

"I hope someone like me is what Jason is looking for," I said. "But you do look very nice. Your hair suits you like that."

She smiled happily. "I think I look great," she said. "Now all you have to do on the way there is tell me what people at the country club talk about."

"Tennis, sailing, music," I said, remembering how I had taken all those conversations for granted.

She made a face. "I don't know a thing about any of that stuff," she said.

"Then talk about what you like," I said. "Not everyone in the world has to like tennis or sailing. Even the most yuppified kids like regular music, you know – and ice cream and desserts. You're an expert on those."

"I can't talk to Jason about ice cream," she said, grabbing on to my arm as if I were a lifeline someone had thrown to her. "You will help me out, won't you, Debbie?"

"I'll do my best," I said, "but I can hardly dance next to you all evening, can I? Just act natural, Ashley. Talk about things you know."

"You don't know Jason," she said, and sighed. "He's clever. He goes to Bronson Academy, and you have to be clever to get in there. I bet he knows about lots of things. I'm going to seem like an idiot."

She was still clutching my arm as we went into Jupiter. I'd only been in there once before – I'm not that wild about loud music – and the music was just as loud as I remembered it. You could feel the floor vibrating. Flashing lights sent bands of colour over the ceiling and walls, painting the faces of the people who were dancing. It was hard to see who was who, so we found ourselves a little table close to the door. That way we could spot Jason if he came in.

The dance ended and a lot of couples made their way back to their tables. Ashley leaped up and gave a little squeak of delight. "There he is," she yelled. "Jason, over here!"

A tall fair boy, skinny and serious looking, turned round, looked at Ashley, then past her, then did a double take. "Ashley?" he asked. "I didn't recognize you. You look so different."

"Yes, well, I like to experiment with different styles," she said in a slightly phony tone. "But this is just my regular old stuff. You know, that I'm comfortable in."

"It's very nice," he said. "I thought that outfit last week was really great too, though."

"Are you alone?" she asked.

"I'm with my friend Roger again," he said. "Remember him from last week? Do you want to come over and join us?"

"Sure," Ashley said. "Uh, this is my friend Debbie. Do you two know each other? She used to live at the Country Club Estates."

Jason looked over at me. "I haven't been in the area too long," he said. "We just moved here from Dallas."

"Oh, wow, Dallas. Like with J. R. and all those oilmen?" Ashley asked happily.

Jason smiled. "My dad's an oilman," he said, "but not anything like J. R."

"See, what did I tell you?" Ashley whispered, giving me a dig in the ribs as we followed Jason across the floor. "His father's in oil!"

"Isn't this cosy?" she asked as we sat at their little corner table. Roger volunteered to get drinks for us, and we were left alone with Jason. We grinned at each other awkwardly while we all thought of something to say, and I wished I could melt through the floor.

"How's your telephone coming along?" Jason asked, clearing his throat nervously.

"My telephone?"

"Yes, you said it was out of order last week."

"Oh, my telephone," she said. "It's still out of order."

"Gee, that's too bad," he said. "You should call up the phone company and complain about their bad service."

"We can't call them up," Ashley said hastily. "Our phone's not working."

Jason laughed, "then I'll just have to drive over and visit you some time," he said.

"No! Don't do that!" Ashley squeaked.

Jason's face clouded. "You don't want me to visit you?"

"Yes … uh, no … I mean, I would like to see you, but my stepfather works nights and sleeps days, so we all have to be very quiet."

"Then I'll come over in the evening, when he's gone."

"No! My mom works days and sleeps nights. I live in a real crazy household," she said. "And their work is top secret."

"Oh really?" he asked. "What sort of top secret, or am I not allowed to ask?"

"Don't ask," she said. "It's so top secret that I don't even know. I just know when they leave the house and come back, and I'm not supposed to ask questions."

"How exciting," Jason said. "I never dated the daughter of spies before."

"Oh, they're not spies," Ashley said, looking around nervously. "They're top secret, er, fashion designers."

"Fashion designers?" he asked. "You mean they design top secret fashions at home? You live in a studio? Then why does one work nights and one days?"

"So they don't get in each other's way and steal each other's ideas," Ashley babbled.

"But surely," Jason began, his forehead wrinkled as he tried to concentrate on the nonsense Ashley was spouting, "it would make more sense if—"

"I'm really not allowed to talk about it," Ashley said, her cheeks bright red by now. "My mom would kill me if she knew I'd told anybody." She gave me another hefty nudge in the ribs. "Get me out of this," she whispered.

"So tell me, Jason," I interrupted. "Do you like this type of music?"

"It's okay," he said. "I like it to dance to. But really I prefer more classical stuff."

"Like Barry Manilow, you mean?" Ashley asked.

He laughed again. "Do you like classical music too?" he asked.

"Me? Oh yes," she said.

"Who's your favourite composer?" he asked.

She looked across at me. "Oh, I like a whole bunch of them," she said, waiting for me to give her a lead. "Let's see, there's . . ."

"Bach," I muttered into my napkin.

"What?"

"Bach," I said louder.

"Woof, woof," Ashley said, surprised.

"What?" Jason asked.

Ashley looked confused. "I was barking," she said.

Jason also looked bewildered for a moment, then his face lit up with understanding. "Oh, I get it. It's a game, right? You were doing Bach, right? Okay, let me think of one."

Mercifully the music began again before we had to suffer through any more embarrassing Guess-the-Composer games. Jason asked Ashley to dance. Roger was also out there, dancing wildly with a girl I didn't know. I sat alone in the corner, feeling like, a wallflower. I remembered what it was like before I had a boyfriend. You sat in corners, pretending you weren't interested in dancing, half hoping that someone would ask you and half hoping they wouldn't. Did I really want to go through all that again?

Ashley and Jason clearly needed no help from me. Out on the dance floor, where they didn't have to worry about making conversation, they got along just fine. I realized suddenly that I was trapped for a whole evening of this, unless Ashley let Jason drive her home tonight. I sipped my drink very slowly, thinking gloomy thoughts. A couple of creepy guys came up and asked me to dance, and I told them I'd sprained my ankle. The future definitely did not look promising.

When a third guy hovered over me, I pretended to be very

interested in folding my napkin into sixteen equal squares. But he didn't seem to get the hint. I was conscious of his big form, looming right over me. In the end I looked up in annoyance.

"Look, buddy, don't you get the message?" I demanded. "I'm just waiting for somebody. I'm not interested in—" My voice failed as I recognized who I was talking to.

A big smile of recognition spread across his handsome face. "I thought it was you sitting there," he said.

I managed a smile of my own. "Hi, Grant," I said. "How have you been?"

Chapter Nine

The music went on playing, and we just kept looking at each other as if we were both seeing ghosts who had materialized unexpectedly. He was even more good-looking than I remembered – he seemed to have have put on a little muscle over the summer, and his tan showing through the open neck of his white knitted shirt … wow! He look like a walking advertisement for Club Med!

"Where did you get that tan?" I blurted out before I remembered that Grant didn't need any help in the ego-boosting department.

"I've been playing a lot of tennis," he said, "and I was up at the cabin on the lake for about a month."

"Oh yes, the lake," I said, remembering that it was his plan to take another girl up there that had contributed to our break-up. "And how was Minda?" I wouldn't have dared ask a question like that before. I had always been rather in awe of Grant. But my time dating Joe had made me more sure of myself and a lot less worried about what people thought.

He grinned, awkwardly. "She, er, didn't come," he said. "I was up there alone. I did a lot of fishing and read about a zillion books."

"And got a great tan," I said. "Well, at least the time wasn't wasted. Think how you're going to impress all those pale girls at Harvard."

"Yeah, Harvard," he said. "Do you realize I'm leaving in just two weeks?"

"It's hard to believe," I said. "The summer's almost over.

He was still standing, holding on to the back of the chair opposite me. "Do you mind if I sit down?" he asked, reminding me how formal our world used to be. "Or are you expecting someone else?" he added.

I waved to the chair. "I'm only here to lend a girlfriend moral support, and it doesn't look as if she needs any," I said. "That's her with her head on the tall fair guy's shoulder."

He looked round. "Oh, I see," he said. "I thought that maybe you were here with, er, what's-his-name."

"What's-his-name and I had a little fight," I said. "I'm not sure if I'm going to forgive him or not."

I saw his eyes react and felt a jolt of excitement that he was still interested in me. "Oh really?" he said. "So you're not going with him at the moment?"

"Not at the moment," I answered. "Maybe never again. I don't think we'll be seeing much more of each other. The cafe is closing."

"Finally condemned?" he asked, laughing as if he had made a good joke.

"It's been sold to developers," I said. "They are putting in a Paradise Inn resort down at Rockley."

"I heard rumours about that," he said. "Good idea, don't you think? That place needed up-grading. And it'll be nice to have tennis courts down at the beach." He looked over at me with sudden interest. "Are you playing much tennis these days?"

"Oh, sure," I said, "What with working five hours a day at the cafe and all the access I have to tennis courts, I should be ready for Wimbledon any minute."

For a moment he looked confused and I felt bad for a second. Obviously he wasn't used to the kind of verbal sparring I'd taken for granted with Joe. Grant finally realized that I was being sarcastic and smiled nervously.

"But you are going to try for the tennis team again at school, aren't you?" he asked.

"I don't know any more," I said, looking down at the tabletop. I traced a line in the design with my finger. "I'd hate to go back and be worse than all the others."

"But you have to try at least," he said firmly. "You were so good. You had real potential, Debbie. You might even attract some college scholarships."

"Might have," I said. "In the past tense. You can't be a good player unless you can practice daily, and I can't anymore."

"I'd really like to help out," he said. "I've got two weeks with nothing to do. Would you like some intensive coaching? I could get you in shape for try-outs."

"Oh, wow, Grant, that would be great!" I said. "Are you sure you have the time?"

He looked a little embarrassed. "Frankly, I'd be glad to have something to take my mind off Harvard," he said. "It's such a big step, and I'm only just beginning to realize that I'll be competing against the best of the best. It's pretty overwhelming when you brood about it."

"In that case," I said, "I'd really appreciate the help."

"Great," he said. "What about this weekend?"

"Fine, but it has to be when I'm not working," I said. "Weekends are our busy times."

A look of annoyance flashed across his face, and I remembered that he hated not getting his own way. "I thought the place was closing."

"It is," I said, "But we haven't been given a date yet."

"Why don't you just quit?"

"I can't just walk out," I said. "There's a whole bunch of people who need me."

"I thought your tennis was important to you," he said.

"It is, but you know me, I hate being unreliable. It's just one of those things I think is really important," I said with great emphasis. "I like to know where I stand with people, and I don't just walk out on them."

He grinned. "Sounds as if the famous boyfriend has been doing things behind your back," he said.

"He has, but not what you think," I said. "He went ahead and sold the cafe without telling anyone."

"Sounds like a smart move to me," Grant said. "And it will be a blessing in disguise for you, too. You'll need more time to yourself in senior year."

"I'll also need money to get myself through college," I said.

"Maybe if we can get your tennis back to its old level, you'll get a scholarship and you won't have to work," he said.

I sighed. "Wouldn't that be wonderful," I said. "I certainly don't look forward to finding another job."

"I could probably help you there, too, if you wanted me to,"

Grant said. "My folks have tons of contacts, remember? But only if you want me to!" he added, grinning. I had once been very angry because he found a nonexistent job for me to get me out of the Heartbreak.

"Thanks," I said. "I might even take you up on it this time. And the tennis definitely. I'd really love to start this weekend. Maybe I can get Joe or Pam to cover for me. Tomorrow morning, maybe?"

"I'm caddying for my father tomorrow," he said. "But Sunday morning would be great."

"I'll try for Sunday then," I said. "That should be fine. We don't open until eleven anyway, so I'm sure someone could cover for me until noon."

"Great," he said, and beamed at me as if I'd just offered him a present.

The music switched from a slow number to a very fast one, and the whole room began to vibrate again. Grant put his hands over his ears. "Do you like this stuff?" he yelled.

"No," I yelled back.

"Then let's go," he shouted.

I looked around for Ashley. She and Jason were still dancing together. Ashley said something and Jason laughed loudly. She didn't appear to be having any problems figuring out the right thing to say to him.

Grant took my arm. "You friend's doing fine," he said. "Let's go somewhere quieter and talk. We've got a lot of catching up to do."

I braved the flying arms and twisting bodies to reach Ashley in the middle of the dance floor. "Ashley, I'm leaving. You obviously don't need me anymore, do you?" I tried to say in her ear as her head jerked up and down.

"Okay," she said without taking her eyes off Jason for a second. I wasn't sure she'd heard, but I was sure that I wasn't needed to get her home. At least this would force Ashley to tell the truth about where she lived, I thought. She'd have to do it sometime if she wanted to become friends with Jason. The thought struck me that maybe Grant was there with somebody too. "Did you come here alone?" I asked.

He made a face. "No, but the group I came with is boring," he said. "Still in high school. So juvenile – all excited about who'll be head cheerleader! I'd much rather to talk to you, Debbie."

"Okay, let's go," I said. "My car's outside, how about yours?"

"Let's go in yours," he said. "I'll get one of my friends to drive mine home for me." He fished out a bunch of keys and jangled them as he walked over to a group all dancing together in the middle of the floor. I saw him wave the keys in front of a girl's face, then press them into her hand.

"Come on, let's go," he said, coming back and taking me by the elbow and steering me out into the night.

We went to Numero Uno and talked until they started sweeping the floor around us at midnight. I think it was probably the first time we'd ever really talked, with me right in the conversation instead of just listening to Grant's view of the world. I noticed he was a little surprised when I interrupted him or disagreed with him, but he didn't seem upset.

"You've grown up a lot in a few months, Debbie," he said. "You were so sheltered before. I hate to say it, but this stint in the sweatshop has done you some good."

"Thank you," I said. "I know I've learned a lot."

"Really?" he asked, seeming to read more meaning into that phrase than I had first intended. I grinned to myself. "Oh yes," I said. "I can hardly believe how far I've come in a few months. But then, Joe's been a good teacher."

I was remembering now the details of our break-up, the going behind my back, the interest in a girl who was more wordly and experienced than me. It was rather nice to give Grant something to think about, to let him know very clearly that the summer had not been wasted without him, that I had learned more than he could ever have taught me.

The moment passed, and we moved on to more ordinary topics – what classes I was taking in senior year, how difficult the senior honours English teacher was, whether Grant could handle chemistry at Harvard. I noticed that he had also matured. Grant would never have admitted before that he might not be ready to handle something, or that he was scared. It made me look at him in a new light, as if he had turned from hero into friend.

When they finally came and told us that they were closing, I drove Grant home. I wondered if he'd try anything in the car, or even invite me in, but he behaved like a perfect gentleman. He didn't even try to kiss me when we pulled up in his driveway.

"I'll call tomorrow and arrange for a court on Sunday. It'll have to be early anyway – you know how crowded it is at the club at weekends. But I think my dad can pull some strings to keep a court for us."

I beamed at myself in the car mirror as I drove off. It was nice to have someone as handsome as Grant interested in me again.

And it would be great to get back to tennis. I felt as if a door had been opened for me and the future was full of possibilities for the first time in ages. Not that I was thinking of a romantic future for me and Grant. After all, he was only going to be home for two more weeks, and besides, I didn't think I felt that way about him anymore. Nor had he shown any indication that he felt that way about me. We were just old friends meeting and sharing what we used to have in common. More than anything, he was showing me that life did not have to end with the closing of the Heartbreak.

Chapter Ten

I was singing to myself as I swung my little car into the garage. Even the difference between Grant's large fake-Tudor house, not unlike the house we used to own a couple of fairways down the golf course, and our present row of bleak condos didn't spoil my mood. In fact, I don't think I even made more than a fleeting comparison. All my feelings were entirely positive: things had been pretty bad and I had worked my tail off all summer at a crummy cafe, but now everything was about to get better again. I was going to play tennis with Grant. I'd get back to my old form, maybe even be captain of the team. Maybe I'd even get a college scholarship and not need to spend my spare time up to my elbows in washing-up liquid.

As I pulled into my parking space, I thought I saw something move in the shadows behind my mother's car. For a moment I remained frozen at the wheel. My mother had always warned me to be careful coming home late at night. You never knew who might be hanging around a big condo development like this. I sat there with the engine running, wondering what I should do. Had I really seen something? Was someone really crouching there behind Mom's car? If so, should I get out and make a dash for my front door?

It was pretty late, well after midnight, and nobody in the

complex was likely to be awake. I kept watching the shadows, waiting for another hint of movement. Suddenly I remembered that Joe had waited for me in the garage once before, when he had been worried about me. He hadn't said anything about my going to the disco with Ashley, but I knew he was pretty angry about it. If he had come to check on my safety, that was a pretty sweet thing to do. For a second, I felt all warm inside.

I opened the car door cautiously. "Joe, is that you?" I asked.

A figure rose from the shadows and began to come round the bonnet of my mother's car. The briefest glance told me that it wasn't Joe. It had wild hair that obscured its face, and it came at me, waving both arms like something out of *Nightmare on Elm Street*. You've never seen anyone switch into reverse so quickly! As I started to back out of the garage, the figure made a lunge towards the car. It was hammering on my window. I was almost out of the parking space and away before it began to register in my panicked brain that it was calling my name in a voice I knew.

I stopped and rolled down the window. "Debbie, don't go, please don't go," the mysterious figure was shouting over the noise of the engine. I switched it off and peered into the darkness.

"Ashley?" I asked incredulously. "Is that you?"

When she pushed back all that hair from her face, I could see that it was.

"What are you doing here?" I asked in horror. "Is something wrong?? Didn't Jason drive you home?"

"Of course he drove me home."

"Did he come on too strong in the car?" I asked. That would explain why she didn't look too great.

"Oh, no," she said quickly. "He was very nice. He only kissed me once, very properly, when I got out."

"So what are you doing here?" I asked, the tension making me shout louder than I intended.

She reacted to my voice, her eyes flashing in fear. "You're not angry with me, are you?" she asked.

"Of course I'm not angry with you," I shouted.

"You sound angry."

I swallowed hard. "I am not angry. Look, Ashley, if you're in some sort of trouble, I'm glad you felt you could come here. Now, would you please tell me what's the matter and how I can help you."

Ashley looked embarrassed. "I need a ride home," she said. "I was wondering if you could drive me."

"Come again?" I asked. "A ride home? Ashley, you just said Jason drove you home."

"Yes, well, you see …" she stammered. "He drove me home, but I, er, I couldn't let him drive me to my crummy block, so I asked him to drive me up to Country Club Estates and I told him to stop outside some big fancy house on Fairway Drive."

"Ashley, you didn't!" I blurted out. "What on earth for?"

She retreated behind her hair. "Because I didn't think he'd still like me if he knew where I really lived," she said softly. "I pretended to walk up the front path, and you couldn't see the front door from the street, so I hid in the bushes and waited until he had left. Then I started to walk home, but I realized I'd never make it all the way. So I stopped off here. I hope you're not really angry."

"I'm not angry with you for wanting a ride home," I said, "But I do think you're crazy to deceive Jason like that. He seems like such a nice guy, and you two were getting along so well. Why would he care if you live on Fairway Drive or down on Market Street?"

"He just might," she said. "He's used to kids from the country club. He talked about all the things you said he'd talk about – you know, tennis and sailing and stuff like plays and Shakespeare. I had to be so careful what I said."

"But how are you going to get out of this?" I asked. "What if he shows up at the front door of that house on Fairway Drive and wants to see you? What if he knows the person who really lives there? Has he asked to see you again?"

"I thought that one out," she said. "I told him I'd meet him at the beach tomorrow. Everyone's the same at the beach, aren't they?"

"You'll have to tell him the truth soon, you know," I said.

She nodded. "I know," she said, "but I'm hoping to wait until he really, truly likes me for myself."

"You're crazy, you know that," I said. "Come on, hop in and I'll drive you home."

"Thanks, Debbie, you're the greatest," she said, running round to the passenger side. "I didn't see you leave tonight," she said as I pulled out onto the street. "What happened."

"I met a friend," I said, and found myself smiling in the darkness.

The next day I said casually to Joe, "Oh, by the way, can you cover for me if I don't show up for work until noon tomorrow, or do you want me to see if Pam can come in?"

I saw his eyes take on a wary look. "Tomorrow's Sunday," he said. "You know we're always busy on Sundays."

"I know," I said, "that's why I asked if you wanted Pam to come in to help get the cafe opened up."

He shrugged to show me he didn't care either way. "I guess we can cope," he said. "Poppa was planning to be in for the day. He's got to do an inventory of all the stuff in here. I don't suppose it would hurt him to cut up a few tomatoes as well."

"Thanks," I said. "I should be in by noon at the latest."

It occurred to me that we were speaking to each other politely, like fellow employees, that we had already moved the first few steps apart, preparing for the separation that was going to follow. And I felt kind of hollow inside, the sort of sadness you feel at the end of a vacation or after a pet dies. Something special had been lost and could never be replaced.

"What's going on tomorrow – are you finally going to church?" Joe asked, breaking into my thoughts as he grinned at me. "It's about time. Think of all those sins you have to confess."

"I am not going to church," I said frostily. As part of a large, Italian Catholic family, Joe's life seemed to be centered round his church. Priests were always dropping in for visits and some relative was always making First Communion or becoming a nun. This was all foreign to me, but for Joe it was all a normal part of everyday life.

"If you must know," I said airly, "Grant's back from the lake and he's going to help me with my tennis."

Joe couldn't mask his reaction. "Oh, Grant's back from the lake," he mimicked. "How very jolly for you. How positively thrilling."

I glared at him. "I don't see what's so funny about it," I said.

"I just thought you'd grown up a bit," he said, turning away from me to start unloading glasses from the dishwasher. "I thought you'd got past your android stage."

"He's only giving me tennis lessons," I said. "Nothing more. I need help from somebody, or I'm not even going to make the team."

"My backhand lob's a little rusty at the moment or I'd offer to help you myself," he said, still mimicking how he thought Grant sounded.

I went on frowning. "Look," I said, "it's really important to me to make the tennis team. I could get a college scholarship maybe. How else am I going to pay for my education? I don't have any old buildings waiting to sell to developers."

"Fine," he said, still with his back to me. "Go ahead and have your tennis lessons with Grant. It doesn't worry me. I guess I can handle two people's work. I have for years."

"Don't try to hit me with a guilt trip," I snapped. "Remember all those times I filled in for you when Wendy needed you to go shopping with her?"

"Oh yes, Wendy," he said smoothly. "I hear Wendy's back from Paris. Maybe I could give her some lessons. Not tennis though. I don't think tennis is her racquet!" And he laughed at his own dumb joke.

"You are so childish!" I said angrily.

"What do you care what I do with Wendy?" he demanded.

"You've made it very clear that you and me don't exist as a couple anymore."

"'You and I,'" I corrected. "We're subjects."

"Oh, I see, now that Grant's back, we have to watch our grammar again," he said with mock sweetness. "I really thought you'd learned that what a person means is more important than how they say it, but I guess once a snob, always a snob."

"I am not a snob," I said fiercely.

"Oh, no? Then what are you? I thought only snobs' kids play in tennis teams and worry about grammar and like to be with androids. How about yuppie then – does junior yuppie fit any better?"

"This conversation is going nowhere," I said.

"Like you and me," he said. "Oh, excuse me – you and I." He took out the last glass and closed the dishwasher with a thump. "It was dumb of me to think we ever belonged together, wasn't it?" he asked. "We live on different planets. There's no way we'd ever make it work, is there?"

"I guess not," I said.

"Right," he said with a big sigh. "So I'll cover for you tomorrow morning. But I hope the android's only got tennis on his mind. You can never totally trust androids, you know. Something in their programming always goes beserk when you least expect it. You'd better watch his backhand!"

"You're being juvenile again," I said with great dignity, and went into the cafe to wipe the tables.

Chapter Eleven

I could tell it was going to be a perfect day, weatherwise, as Grant drove me up to the country club early on Sunday morning. Thin ribbons of mist curled up from the ocean, and above was a clear pearly sky, bright with promise of warm sunshine. Sitting beside me, Grant looked even more handsome than on Friday night, his tennis whites accenting his perfect, even tan, his hair sunstreaked, and little laugh lines crinkling round his eyes. I sighed happily. I was going to play tennis again, get back the form I had lost. I was going back to the country club and all my old friends, who I had hardly seen for months. And yet, as we turned up the hill toward the clubhouse and the courts, my stomach began to tie itself in knots. I was coming back as an outsider, no longer someone who belonged there. Would my former friends make me welcome, or was I making a mistake in believing that I could pick up my old life where I'd left off?

I tried to look cool and casual as I strode out with Grant to our court. A few people recognized me and did a double take at seeing me there.

"Why Debbie," a friend's mother said, "you're back. How nice to see you again. How are your parents?" And she waited for me to fill her in on whether I was back alone or whether my parents were possibly back together as a unit. When I told her my mother was just fine and my father had gone to a writer's workshop for the summer, she nodded and repeated that it was good to see me again.

My tennis was better than I had feared. The timing on my serve was off, but apart from that I was only a little rusty. The long hours on my feet all summer had even toughened up my leg muscles. Grant seemed pleased with me.

"We'll have you back in top form in no time at all," he said, and put me through a grueling work-out.

I was so tired that I could scarcely crawl into the Heartbreak at noon. Even a long soak in the tub when I got home didn't do much to ease all those overworked shoulder and arm muscles. My mother fussed around me, not able to conceal her delight.

"So you and Grant are playing tennis together again?" she asked. "Did you have a good game?"

"Pretty good."

"And how is Grant? I guess he leaves for Harvard fairly soon."

She was treading cautiously, I could tell. She didn't want to come right out and say how delighted she was that I was now mixing with the right sort of kids again, but it was obvious. Clearly she thought that my episode down at the Heartbreak was one of those unfortunate periods parents have to go through, but now I would be back to normal. I was glad she was so confident that I'd now sorted out my life, because I was not at all sure about what I wanted or where I was going. I did know, after two hours on the tennis court, that I wanted to get back in shape for tennis again. I really wanted to make that team, and not just slip in as an alternate either. I was aiming for captain.

Luckily Pam was there when I arrived at the Heartbreak.

"Joe said you might be late, so I came in early," she said. "What were you doing? Joe was being mysterious about it."

"Nothing mysterious," I said. "I merely went for some tennis coaching with Grant."

"Grant?" she exclaimed. "What's he doing here? I thought he was already off at Harvard."

"Not for two more weeks. He's offered to help me get in shape for the tennis team."

Pam grinned. "No wonder Joe was so grouchy."

"I don't know what he's got to be grouchy about," I said. "He said himself that he and I are history."

Pam kept on grinning. "He doesn't mean that any more than you do," she said.

"I'm totally serious," I said. "We've had our little fights in the past, but this one is too big to patch up. Besides, when the Heartbreak goes we'll have nothing to keep us together, even if that's what we wanted, which we don't."

"Too bad," Pam said. "I thought you made a terrific couple." Then she saw my face and added quickly, "Besides, you and Joe provided the main entertainment in my life. I hope you won't go back to Grant – listening to your life together was like reading the Who's Who of High School Students: very boring."

"I'm only interested in tennis, thank you," I said. "I've had enough emotional upheavals in my life recently without adding the complication of someone who's going to leave for college in two weeks."

Joe walked in just then. "Anyone for tennis?" he asked sweetly, and struck a ridiculous pose.

A week ago I would have laughed, but now I was no longer

prepared to be amused, impressed, or in any way approving of anything he did.

"I doubt if you'd know a lob from a volley," I said.

"Maybe not, but some people say I'm famous for my love games," he said, giving Pam a wink.

"And some people would say you're famous for your backhand slices," I shot back. I turned deliberately to Pam. "As I was saying, I had a great time. I'd forgotten how sweet Grant really is. And he's a total gentleman. He's offered to devote every minute from now until he leaves to getting my tennis back to where it was."

"On a tennis court?" Joe quipped.

"He even talked about playing in a doubles tournament together," I went on, ignoring him very successfully.

"Oh how lovely, rainbow tennis," Joe joked. "Blue blood and green blood on the same court."

"I'll tell you the rest later, Pam," I said. "I can't talk with these constant childish interruptions."

Joe shot me a black look and flung some hamburger patties onto the grill. "Would it be too much to ask you to put on your uniform and get to work?" he asked. "Or has tennis exhausted you for the day?"

"Don't worry, I plan to do my share of work," I said. "I guess I can stand anything for a week or so longer." I took my uniform out of the cupboard and hung up my bag. "So tell me, have your friends in the demolition business set a date for bulldozing this place yet?" I asked. "I only want to know because I'd hate to be changing in the cloakroom when a bulldozer comes in through the wall."

"Don't worry, he'd back right out again," Joe said. "Bulldozer men are known for their weak stomachs."

"Very amusing," I said coldly.

"And no, they haven't set a date yet," he said, grinning at having scored a point. "Everything's been put on hold. There seems to be some problem with the environmental impact report. They told us it was only a formality, but apparently some weirdo ecology group has requested a study of the wildlife in the area before they issue permits for a high rise."

"How dumb of them," I said. "After all, what could a few hundred seals and birds possibly matter if a bunch of kids in a cafe don't matter?"

Joe scowled at me and turned back to his hamburgers, just in time to see one of them sliding down the grill toward the sink. He caught it as it was about to disappear.

I couldn't resist the parting shot. "Never did get the hang of that, did you?" I asked. "Well, you don't have to worry now. Cooking hamburgers is almost a thing of the past."

Strangely, I could say things like that to him, fight an ongoing battle on a purely verbal level, with my emotions firmly shut off. I think that deep down I felt that by hurting him, I'd somehow ease my own hurt.

The battle went on all week. Every time I came in after my early tennis with Grant, Joe had thought up new twists on his insult campaign, which only made Grant seem better and better in my eyes. As I told Pam, he was a perfect gentleman. He was very patient with my tennis, he was constantly encouraging, and he never teased or insulted me.

"What a change after putting up with Mr Wisecrack here for

all these months," I said to Pam. "At least with Grant, if he says something, he really means it."

We played for two hours every morning, and I began to feel really confident about the tennis team. I was channeling all my aggression and anger about things at the cafe into my tennis strokes and it showed.

"You're hitting the ball harder than ever," Grant commented, not knowing that each tennis ball I whacked had Joe's name written invisibly across it. Grant fell into step beside me as we walked from the court. "I wish we'd got together sooner this summer," he said. "Instead of just the regular club tournaments, we could have entered the junior mixed doubles open."

"Did you enter with someone else?" I asked. He shook his head. "I couldn't think of anyone good enough to partner me. And anyway, I was still up at the lake."

We walked down the six steps from the court to the locker rooms. "It's been really beautiful up there this summer," he said. "Do you ever get any time off from your greasy spoon job?"

"I get two days a week," I said. "I've been taking Monday and Tuesday, but it's really flexible. Pam and I swap round."

"I was thinking of going up there once more, before I head for the hard slog of Harvard," he said. "One final escape to get my head together. Want to come?"

"To the lake?" I asked, my voice betraying my surprise.

"Sure," he said. "I bet you could use a break, too, couldn't you?"

I was caught entirely off guard. I guess I wasn't prepared to make the switch from Grant the tennis coach to a Grant who wanted to take me to the lake with him. I remembered Minda and all the connotations of 'going to the cabin at the lake.'

"I, er, just for the day, you mean?" I blurted out, trying to read his face.

He was still walking along, swinging his tennis racquet at the geranium heads along the path and looking totally relaxed, as if he were inviting me to go with him for a soda.

"It's a long drive," he said. "Better to spend the night up there."

"Oh," I said, sounding like a total idiot. "Spend the night, huh?"

"My parents will be up there, too," he said with a little sideways grin at me. "You don't have to worry."

"I'm not worrying," I said quickly.

"I could stand some company on the ride up," he said. "And if you're there, my father won't make me go fishing with him."

"I'd have to ask my mother," I said. "She's kind of old-fashioned about me going up to lake cabins with boys."

"I'll come over and ask her myself if you like," he said. "She knows my parents and she used to like me."

"She still does," I said with a grimace. "She couldn't stop dancing round the kitchen when she heard that you and I were playing tennis together. Parents are so childish, aren't they?" I knew I was babbling, but I was buying myself time because I wasn't sure whether I wanted to go to the lake with him or not. I was still trying to read his face, but he wasn't looking directly at me. He seemed so cool and relaxed that I decided I was panicking for no reason.

"I'm sure there won't be any problem," I said. "As you said, I really could use a break. I haven't been away all summer, except to my father's a couple of times."

"Is he still living down at Whitney Cove?" he asked, looking at me, I thought, with pity.

I nodded. "Except right now he's up at a mountain retreat for writers," I said. "He's hoping to write the great American screenplay in a month."

Grant shook his head. "I still can't think of your father as a drop-out," he said. "The image I have of him is still in a business suit with a briefcase under his arm." He looked at me with understanding. "This year has been something else for you, hasn't it?"

"You can say that again," I said. "I feel like *Alice in Wonderland.* I keep wondering which rabbit hole I'm going to fall down next."

"It must have been nice to be back with your friends in the old surroundings this week," he commented.

"Oh sure," I said. Afterwards, showering alone in the girl's locker room, I gave this some thought. It had been wonderful to be back at tennis, to feel the power in my swing and to know that I hadn't lost it all. But coming back was also tinged with sadness – like a child being allowed to play with a toy for a little while and then having it taken away again. Surely Grant must have seen that being back at the club couldn't help opening old wounds for me?

We really did live in different worlds now, I thought. I didn't think it even entered his head that it must be difficult for me to come back as an outsider ... but then, that was Grant for you. He never was strong on putting himself in someone else's position. But he was trying – had to admit that. He was more considerate than when we used to date. Maybe he had grown up this summer, too.

I paused and towel-dried my hair fiercely. Was he asking me up to the lake because he felt sorry for me? I wondered. Were the tennis lessons and the trip to the lake his good deeds before he went off to college? In which case he *had* changed a lot over the summer. More likely it was just as he'd said – he was only inviting me because he hated driving up there alone. Well, at least I didn't have to worry about him trying anything if I was only someone to talk to on the drive up there. And his parents would be there. And I'd make it very clear to him that I was only interested in him as a tennis partner. Besides, I really did need a break, *and, more than anything, I couldn't wait to see Joe's face when he heard about it!*

Chapter Twelve

My mother, as I'd suspected, put up no objections to my going with Grant to the lake.

"How very nice of him to ask you," she said.

"You don't mind?" I asked. "I remember when you'd have been very against it."

"Things have changed," she said. "As you keep telling me, you have matured and I can trust you. I do trust you, Debbie. And beyond that, if Grant's parents are there, then I know you'll be well supervised. We've known his parents for a long time. I worked with his mother on the Symphony Ball one year. That was the year we had all those arches of balloons ... They were so pretty ... pink and white ..." Her face grew wistful.

"Mom?" I asked. "Do you miss all that very much? The country club and our big house and all the society dances?"

"Not the big house," she said quickly. "Too much cleaning!" And she laughed, as if she wanted to cover up her true feelings. After a pause she added, "But I do miss the social life. When you get to be my age, it's not easy to meet people and make friends."

"You could still do some of that volunteer stuff if you wanted to, couldn't you?" I asked.

She put down her coffee mug. "Volunteering costs money,"

she said. "All those jobs I did for the local theatre and children's hospital and the golf club – they all required a lot of money. Not just expensive dresses for the gala events, but day-to-day money. The person in charge would say, 'Let's each make a dozen table centerpieces,' and those table centers would cost several dollars apiece to make. We never thought much of it in those days. Now it would be impossible."

We both sat for a moment in silence, digesting how much things had changed. I was remembering the conversations I had listened to in the country club locker room all week – girls discussing trips to Europe and condos in Hawaii and shoes that cost a hundred dollars a pair, as if all these things were normal parts of life. I suppose I must have been like that too. At least one thing Joe had helped me to see was the true value of money. Until he turned traitor, that is, and sold out to those developers.

"So how's the newspaper going?" I asked. "Is it really worth not going back to college."

My mother's eyes became wary. "Don't let's start that again, Debbie," she said.

"I wasn't going to," I said. "I've learned that people don't do what you want them to, whatever you say. I was just curious, that's, all."

"It's, er, very interesting," she said. "Of course, I spend a lot of my time doing research for other people, or covering boring stuff like weddings and funerals. For the last few days I've been writing the entire obituary page – not the most thrilling assignment. But Ralph has offered to take me out on some exciting assignments with him."

"How positively thrilling," I said, and made a face. I had never liked Ralph and was glad when the romance between him and my mother fizzled out.

Mom laughed at my expression. "Whatever you think about him, Debbie, he is a good newspaperman. I can learn a lot by watching his technique."

"You'd just better watch his technique, young woman," I said, and we both laughed.

"So does this trip to the lake mean the end of the cafe?" she asked me.

"Not yet," I said. "They have to wait for the environmental impact study first. We're all just hanging on down there, waiting for the axe to fall."

"If you like I could get you a job at the newspaper," she said. "It might be enjoyable for you. I know you weren't interested earlier in the summer, but it would be more varied than fast food."

"Thanks, Mom," I said. "I don't really know what I want to do. I really want to make the tennis team again, so I'll have to see how much time I have left over for work. Grant thinks I might be good enough to get a scholarship, which would mean I wouldn't have to spend my evenings slaving away."

I saw the pain cross her face. "I wanted things to be so different, Debbie," she said. "I never dreamed you'd have to work like this. Your teenage years should be free and happy."

"Oh, I don't mind," I said. "I've really enjoyed working at the Heartbreak. It's been hard, but it's been fun, too. I'll really miss . . ." My voice trailed off. "I'd better go or I'll be late for work," I said.

Joe's reaction to the lake trip was just as I had predicted.

"I thought you said you were just playing tennis with him?" he demanded.

"I was, but now I'm going to Phoenix Lake with him," I said. "I need to get away." I failed to mention to Joe that Grant's parents were going, too.

Joe glowered. "I see," he said coldly. "You fight me off all summer, then you run off to a cosy little cabin with Mr Perfect Android. I guess money must talk for you, too. It must be the car he drives, because it can't be his personality."

"Grant is a very pleasant person," I said. "I know where I stand with him. We're just friends, and we're going to have a couple of relaxing days . . . I don't know why I'm explaining all this to you. I don't have to ask your permission to go to the lake with someone!"

"Just be careful, that's all," Joe growled. "Your Mister Perfect might not be so perfect when he's got you all alone up there."

"You don't know anything about it," I said frostily. "Not all boys have one-track minds like you. Grant needs to relax before college and he wants company. He happens to find my company pleasant, which is more than you do. I have no reservations at all about going to the lake with him."

"Then you're dumber than I thought," Joe said. "But as you said, it's none of my business."

"No, it's not."

"So I can't stop you."

"No, you can't."

"Fine. Enjoy it."

"I will."

"Just don't come crying to me if it doesn't turn out the way you planned."

"Don't worry, I won't."

We stood glaring at each other like two dogs about to fight. Then Joe sighed and turned away.

"Oh, and if they tear down the Heartbreak while I'm gone, please let me know," I called after him. "I really don't want to come in to work on Wednesday morning only to find a big hole and no cafe!"

He turned back to say something, thought better of it, and went out, slamming the door. Joe didn't say any more about the trip to the lake. Only once, as I prepared to go home on Sunday, did he come up behind me.

"I suppose you're still planning to go through with this?" he asked.

"With what?" I replied innocently.

"The orgy at the lake."

"Grow up," I said. "Grant was brought up very well and I'm perfectly safe. Anyway, I can take good care of myself!"

"I sure hope so," Joe said, "I hope I won't have to say I told you so!"

"I don't intend to give you that satisfaction," I said. And I tossed my hair as I walked out.

Chapter Thirteen

The drive up to the lake was beautiful. We soon left all traces of civilization behind and began to wind our way up through the mountains. Since it was a warm day, we had all the car windows open, letting in the sweet herby smells of the shrubs growing beside the road. I let one arm trail outside the car, feeling the wind play with my fingers, while Grant drummed his fingers on the steering wheel in time with the music on the radio. Occasionally he looked over at me and smiled.

"Feeling okay?" he asked. "Not car sick?"

"Just fine thanks."

"Some people get car sick from going round all these bends."

"You're a good driver. The car hardly sways at all."

"I've had a lot of practice on this road," he said, smiling at the compliment, "but I admit, I do handle this car well. From the moment I got it, it was as if we were made for each other."

"A match in a car factory in Germany," I quipped.

He smiled, but I could tell he hadn't really understood, or maybe he hadn't been listening. I realized again that he wasn't like Joe. Conversations with Grant didn't have to be peppered with word play and verbal point scoring.

"Do you want to go water skiing this afternoon?" he asked.

"Or maybe we should just relax and unwind today and do the water skiing in the morning when the lake is calmer."

"Fine with me either way," I said. "This is the first break I've had in goodness knows how long, so I'll be content to just lie there and do nothing."

"Sounds fine to me," he said nodding. "We've got a floating dock that's great for sunbathing. That gentle hobbling motion is so soothing. You can't help relaxing."

"I'm feeling pretty relaxed already," I said, leaning against the headrest of my seat and watching the blue sky pass overhead.

"Good," he said. "I mean, that's what we came here for – to relax-isn't it."

A new tune came on the radio and Grant tapped his fingers in time to it again. I closed my eyes and drifted into a half sleep. When I opened them again, we were descending. The road snaked downward and there, through the pine trees, I saw a glimpse of blue water."

"Not long now," Grant said.

The scent of pines was overpowering now – clean and tangy as if a giant bottle of air freshener had been sprayed over the countryside. Dotted here and there among the trees were little rustic cabins. The trees beside the road thinned and there was the lake, glittering and blue, with mountain peaks rising up around it.

"Wow," I said in awe.

"Pretty, isn't it?" Grant said, sounding as if he had created it just for me. "You wait until you see our cabin. The view from there is really nice."

The road now hugged the lake's edge. We passed a little shop with a gas pump outside and a few small boats docked at a marina behind it. The store had an old-fashioned flashing Coca-Cola sign in the window, a tin board advertising ice cream outside, and inflatable water toys strung up across the doorway. It looked as if no one had changed a thing about it for years.

After the shop, we didn't see any more houses along the lake. After a couple of miles the road moved inland to pass a little peninsula that jutted out on our left. A wall ran along beside the road, cutting off our view of the peninsula beyond, broken in the middle by an imposing brick gateway with curly iron gates.

"Here we are," Grant said. He climbed out and opened one of the gates. We glided through. On the tip of the peninsula a house was perched, all glass and natural wood, following the contour of the rocky shoreline on various levels.

"Some cabin," I muttered. It was nothing like the homey little places we had seen nestled among the trees. In fact, it was more like something you'd see featured on "Lifestyles of the Rich and Famous!"

"My dad got an architect friend to design it for him in return for some stock advice," Grant commented. "It's nice, isn't it?"

"Nice is hardly the word," I said. "It's spectacular." Grant smiled again, looking as if he were personally responsible for producing the house out of a hat like a rabbit.

We came to a halt in a circular gravel driveway. I couldn't help noticing that there were no other cars. "Er, do you have a garage?" I asked.

"A garage? No, just the driveway. We're only really up here in the summer, so a garage wasn't necessary."

"I see. I guess your parents aren't here, then," I said, trying to sound very calm.

"Oh, er, no, they don't seem to be here, do they?" he commented. "I could have sworn they said they were coming up today. Maybe they're out to lunch with friends. They do that a lot."

"Oh yes," I said. "That must be it."

"Come on," he said grinning at me. "I'll show you around."

He went ahead of me, up a couple of polished slate steps, and opened a big front door. It opened on to a large living room that was mostly window. A breathtaking view of lake and mountains took the place of two of the walls. A rough stone fireplace made up most of the third. The floor was also slate, with Indian rugs dotted here and there and low leather furniture. I went over and looked out of the window. The house was designed so that we were actually over the lake, held up on angled posts.

"See, you can go fishing without even leaving the house," Grant said, coming up behind me. "Just dangle a line and the fish will fight for the privilege to be caught first. Very snobby fish in Phoenix Lake – they want to be caught by only the best people."

He laughed and I relaxed again. After all, this was Grant. The Grant I knew so well, who had been my playmate at the country club long before we were interested in each other romantically. If his parents weren't here right now, it was no big thing. I could trust him completely, couldn't I?'

"I'll show you the bedrooms," he said. "We've got a really nice guest room – very private." He led the way down a tiled hallway and opened a door at the end of it. It led along another hallway and into a small white room. It was shady and cool and looked out on trees, not the lake.

"It's got it's own bathroom and everything," he said. "You can really relax here if you want to."

I glanced up and thought I saw a shadow move past the window – just a hint of movement beyond the blinds. I looked again, but nothing was there. Shivering, I said, "I think I like the sun better." Then I blurted, "Are there many wild animals up here?"

"Wild animals?" he asked.

"I thought I saw something go past the window."

He parted the blinds and looked out. "Probably a deer," he said. "There're a lot of them around here. Or maybe it was the shadow of a bird flying over. The birds of prey are pretty big up here – vultures and hawks and even eagles, I understand."

"Let's go back to the living room," I said. "It's cold in here."

"Yes, it's always cool in here," he said. "We really appreciate it on hot afternoons."

He led the way back. "Hungry?" he asked, and took me into a very modern kitchen. "I brought fresh bread and fruit with us, but we keep the fridge well stocked with most other things," he said, opening it to reveal an Aladdin's cave of cold meats, cheeses, yogurts, and drinks.

"Help yourself," he said. "We can take it out to the deck to eat."

I made myself a sandwich and he prepared a tray for us. "What about a glass of wine?" he asked. "I always think it goes very well with lunch. It's very relaxing."

Outside the window there was a noise, like an animal scrabbling.

"Those damned squirrels again," he said. "They do terrible damage to the roof. Want some wine?"

"Just some juice for me," I said. "I don't really drink."

"One glass is totally harmless, you know," he said. "I put lots of ice with it. But there are plenty of juices to choose from if you'd rather."

I took a can of apple juice and followed him out on to a deck, down below the kitchen, almost at lake level. There were several lounge chairs on it, as well as a glass table with some chairs. We sat and ate together. The bread was very fresh, the food delicious, but I couldn't totally relax. It wasn't Grant's presence beside me, or the nagging doubt that perhaps his parents weren't going to be here after all. It was something else, as if eyes were watching me from the forest. Those trees seemed tall and menacing, and I kept seeing movements in the shadows which made me start and turn round, only to see nothing there.

"I don't know why I'm so jumpy," I said. "Does Bigfoot ever show up around here?"

"Nothing like that," Grant said, laughing. "You're just not used to the wonders of nature. Anything up here is totally harmless – just deer, squirrels, occasionally a skunk or a raccoon at night. That's about it." He got to his feet. "Let's get changed into our swimming things. What you need is some sunbathing and swimming."

We went inside and I changed in the cold, dark room, looking out through the blinds several times and wondering why my imagination was working overtime today. When I came out, Grant was already down at the dock. He had spread a towel on an air mattress and was lying facedown in the sun. I went to join him.

"Lie down," he said, "and I'll rub suntan lotion on your back for you. You need a good sunscreen up here – the sun's very fierce up this high." I lay down on my stomach, and he began to rub the cream into my back. It felt good, his strong hands going up and down my back, over my shoulders, down the back of my legs ... I closed my eyes, letting my arms trail over the edge of the dock, my fingertips barely touching the cold water. The only sounds were the gentle lap and slap of water, the sigh of wind in the pine trees, and the lonely cry of a distant bird. I began to feel the tension seeping out of my body.

"Feels good, huh?" Grant asked.

"Great," I murmured.

I moved my hand away as something brushed against it – a little fish nipping at it, maybe. I opened my eyes and found myself looking down over the edge of the dock into Joe's wet face. He had come up underneath the dock, where Grant couldn't see him. Amazingly, I was able to choke back my cry of surprise.

"What's wrong?" Grant asked.

I looked down at Joe's face, his wet curls plastered to his head like a bedraggled puppy. It would be the easiest thing in the world to tell Grant we had an intruder and get him thrown out. I opened my mouth, looked down into Joe's eyes, and closed it again.

"Nothing," I said. "You just touched a ticklish spot, that's all."

"Sorry," he said. "Here, let me finish off the backs of your legs, then you can do me."

"What are you doing here?" I mouthed down to Joe. He grinned. "Fishing," he said. "Under-dock fishing. New sport."

"Go away!"

"What's he doing to you?" Joe whispered, keeping his face just clear of the water.

"Only putting on sunscreen," I mouthed back, hoping that the lapping of the water would mask any sound.

"Not what it looks like to me."

"Will you go away? If you don't I'll tell him you're here!"

"You wouldn't."

"Are you talking to yourself?" Grant asked. "I keep thinking I hear you muttering."

"Just singing to myself," I said. "Water always makes me want to sing." I heard Joe splutter under the dock. "You're done," Grant said, giving my leg a playful slap. "Now you can do me."

"Okay," I said, sitting up. I started to rub on the sunscreen.

"Mmmm, that feels so good," Grant said. "You have great hands. I should get you to give me a massage more often."

"Ow," I yelled as a splash of cold water hit my back.

"What's wrong now?"

"I got splashed," I said. "Must have been a freak wave. Maybe we should go up to the deck. That water really is very cold."

"If you like," Grant said. "Although I think I might go for a quick swim first. Here, you want to try a mask and fins? There are some really interesting things growing around this dock."

"I bet," I said. "But I don't feel in the mood for swimming right now."

I was beginning to wonder if Joe could breathe all right under the dock. What if a large wave came, or the wake from a boat? There could only be a few inches between his face and the water. Of course, it would serve him right if he drowned! What a nerve he had, coming up here to spy on me!

"I have a great idea," I said, getting to my feet. "Why don't we take the boat out. We could go way down the lake; in fact, all around the lake! That way we'd get great tans, and I'd be able to see the entire lake."

"If you like," Grant said. I didn't think he sounded too pleased.

"Does your boat go fast?" I asked. "I love going fast! I bet we can be at the other end of the lake in seconds!"

"Why are you talking so loudly?" Grant asked. "I'm right here."

"Oh, I guess you are," I said, giggling. "Open spaces always make me talk too loud for some reason. Come on, race you up to the boathouse!"

Shortly after that we were down at the other end of the lake, zooming in and out of the little coves. *Let him try and follow me now,* I thought, and I giggled as I imagined Joe swimming for all he was worth as the powerful boat sped across the lake!

When we got back to Grant's house much later that afternoon, after a long boat ride, a swim, and a stop on the way back for ice cream at a funny little fisherman's store at a marina, there was no sign of Joe.

Chapter Fourteen

I changed out of my swimming things in the cold guest room, took a long shower, dried my hair, then went out to join Grant. The big living room was still full of late afternoon sun and felt warm and friendly. Grant was sitting on the windowseat, looking out at the water. He had turned on the radio and soft rock was drifting out. Grant got up when I came in.

"You must be getting hungry," he said. "How about a steak for dinner? My parents always keep really good steaks in the freezer."

"Your parents still don't seem to be here," I commented.

"No . . . they don't do they?" he said, clearing his throat and seeming embarrassed. "I must have got it wrong. I could have sworn they said they were coming up."

It suddenly dawned on me that he'd known all along that they weren't coming. Grant must have noticed the angry look on my face because he went on hurriedly: "They do change their minds sometimes. My father's work is very unpredictable. He probably had to meet a client at the last minute."

"How very convenient of him," I said, fighting to keep my temper in check. It wasn't that I was really worried about being in a cabin alone with Grant – after all, I'd been in his house alone with him millions of times. It was just that it was so childish. *He probably wanted me to go up to the lake and thought that my mother wouldn't let me go if we were going to be alone,* I thought.

"So, it looks as if we're all alone up here," I said.

"I guess so." He laughed, a sort of forced phony laugh. "But don't worry, I'll keep away all the scary animals."

"I thought you said there weren't any."

"There aren't. It's just that . . . well, I noticed you were a little nervous at being up here all alone."

"Who me? Nervous?" I asked. "I'm not nervous."

"That's good," he said. "How about a drink before dinner? I'll put those steaks in the microwave, and we can relax while they're defrosting. Do you want to try the wine now?"

"Er, sure," I said.

"I'll get it," Grant said. "You stay and enjoy the view. This is the very best time of the day."

I curled up on the windowseat and looked out.

"Psst," said a voice right below me. I glanced down, and there was Joe again. As I said, the house was built out over the lake, the living room supported by big diagonal posts jutting out from the rocks on the shore. Joe was now clinging to one of those posts right below the window, his face looking up at me as he clung on crazily.

"Are you still here?" I demanded.

"Now he's trying to get you drunk, isn't he?" Joe demanded. "Just like I thought."

"What a ridiculous thing to say. It's only a glass of wine!"

"A glass can affect you more than you think," he said. "You shouldn't have one."

"Will you mind your own business and go away?"

"I'm just warning you! Isn't it obvious that he set this whole thing up! No parents, relaxing massages, wine. I can read his mind like a book!"

"Just because you think that way—" I began. But then I heard Grant come back into the room.

"Here, take this," Grant said, handing me a very tall glass. I looked at it – it was certainly a lot of wine.

"Crisps," I said as Grant approached the windowseat.

"Do you have any crisps or crackers? I really like to nibble on something when I drink."

"I'll go and get some," Grant said.

"Perfect."

"And then we can sit together on the sofa and watch the sun set. It's the most romantic scene you'll ever see."

Down below I thought I heard Joe sneeze. As soon as Grant had gone, I leaned out the window again.

"Don't sit on the sofa with him!" Joe warned.

"Why not?"

"I don't trust him, that's why!"

"Maybe I want to," I said. "Did it ever occur to you that maybe I came up here because I want to get romantic with Grant again? You said yourself that we were history – did it ever occur to you that I might have known what he had in mind?"

Joe stared at me for a long while before he said, "I don't believe you. You don't feel a thing for that android. You never did."

"Maybe I've changed my mind. Maybe I want to be with a

guy who's more my type, who's honest and reliable. And you don't need to worry about me. I'm sure Grant will know exactly when to stop."

"Hah," Joe said. "They always say the snakes with the smoothest skins are the most dangerous."

"Who always says that?"

"I do. I made that up. Pretty good for a humble guy like me, huh?"

"There's nothing humble about you, Joe Garbarini," I said. We looked at each other for a long minute. I could hear Grant in the kitchen. "Now will you please go?" I asked. "I'm a big girl. I can take care of myself, and I do not want you clinging to that post all night."

"In that case, help me inside," Joe said, starting to pull himself up. "It's freezing cold not to mention wet out here. I'll just hide behind the sofa ... in case you need help."

"You will not!" I said. "Now get out of here before Grant finds you. Go home and leave me alone!"

I hadn't meant to push him so hard. It was supposed to be just a symbolic shove, but his hands were cold and wet and I guess the post was slippery. He lost his balance, flailed for a moment, and then fell backward into the lake. Just then Grant came back in.

"What was that?" he asked. "I thought I heard a splash."

"You did," I said. "I threw something into the lake."

"Oh? What?"

"An ... ice cube. I threw an ice cube from my drink into the lake."

"What on earth for?"

"To watch the ripples. I like to watch them get bigger and bigger."

"Pretty big splash for an ice cube," he said. "I heard it from the kitchen with all the windows closed."

"Well, urm … a fish might have thought it was food, because it jumped right out of the water and fell back again with a big splash," I said. "Wasn't that weird?"

Grant looked at me as if he couldn't figure me out. "You are strange sometimes," he said. "I guess that's one of the things that attracts me to you." He sank on to the leather sofa with his bowl of crisps. "Here, come and sit beside me or we'll miss the sunset."

I came over and sat beside him. We sipped our drinks and watched the sun, now a clearly defined red ball, slip below the horizon until it splashed into the far end of the lake and was gone. It was, as Grant had promised, very romantic. He slipped an arm round my shoulder. "Isn't this great?" he asked. "Just you and me and this beautiful view?"

He was looking down at me, smiling. I nodded. "Great," I said.

"You know," he began meditatively, "when I think of all the time we wasted this summer – time we could have been spending together … I don't know why we broke up. I was so dumb to let you get away. This week has been great, hasn't it?"

I nodded. "It's been fun," I said.

"Did you miss me, too?"

"Sometimes," I said honestly.

"All the time I was alone at the lake, I kept thinking of you," he said. "I wished you were up here with me."

Only because Minda didn't show up, a voice inside me nagged.

"You and I, we make a great couple, don't we?" he asked. "And I don't just mean for tennis."

He turned my face toward his and kissed me, gently, on the lips. It was a tender kiss, but as Joe had predicted, I felt nothing.

"Grant … those steaks should be thawed enough by now, shouldn't they?" I said, moving away from him as soon as I could. "Gee, this lake air makes you hungry. How about a salad to go with them? I'm great at salads."

"Debbie," he said, touching my arm gently. "You don't have to be nervous, honestly. Just relax. Let me get you another glass of wine."

"I've only taken two sips of the first one," I said.

"Then drink up. Lake air is known to make people thirsty, too."

"I'll take it with me and start on the salad," I said, moving ahead of him towards the kitchen. He didn't try to protest this time, but came in with me. He lit the gas grill and threw two large steaks on to it. Relieved, I delved into the fridge and came up with all sorts of salad goodies, which I chopped up with professional skill.

"One of the benefits of working at the Hearbreak," I said, nodding at the counter. "Look how well I can cut up tomatoes."

Grant nodded, then went back to spreading barbeque sauce on the steaks. "So you and Joe aren't seeing each other anymore."

"I wouldn't exactly say that," I said, stifling a giggle. "We bump into each other from time to time."

"I meant dating each other," Grant said. "You're not dating anymore."

"No," I said.

"Good," he said. "He was something else, that Joe, wasn't he?" Grant asked, still not looking up from his cooking.

"That's Joe – something else," I said. I couldn't stop thinking about him now. I hadn't seen him swim away after the splash. *I hope he's okay,* I thought. *I hope he doesn't get too cold and go and catch pneumonia. I hope he goes right home and changes those wet clothes!*

"It must have been a big change for you to date someone like that after me," Grant said casually.

"You can say that again," I said.

"I mean," Grant went on, sounding more as if this were just a monologue and he wasn't even waiting for my replies, "he's so sort of primitive and wild. I bet you had a hard time fighting him off . . . unless you didn't want to fight him off, that is?"

"It's none of your business, Grant," I said. "What Joe and I did was private, between us. I don't like discussing him with other people."

"I guess it was wrong of me to ask you. It's just that . . . well, I get jealous when I think of Joe doing certain things with you – things I would never have dared to do—"

"The salad's ready," I said, cutting him off. "How about the steaks?"

We ate at the round white kitchen table, not saying much. The water had turned pearl grey and by the time we had finished eating, darkness had fallen. One minute it was pinkish twilight, the next there was nothing but blackness outside the windows – no other light for the whole length of the lake.

Grant finished his wine while I just sipped at mine. I was still thinking about Joe, still mad that he had come up here to spy on me, but still worried about him too. *He still thinks he owns me,* I thought, stabbing at a piece of steak with my knife. *If he thinks he's going to follow me around for the rest of his life, he's sadly mistaken.*

We topped off the steak and salad with some chocolate chip ice cream and then went back into the living room. Grant patted the sofa beside him.

"What time is it?" I asked. "Is there anything on TV."

"No TV up here," he said. "This is a total back-to-nature experience."

"A game then," I said, looking around hopefully. "Is that Trivial Pursuits I see under the coffee table? I just love Trivial Pursuits, don't you?" I didn't wait for him to answer as I pulled it out and started opening up the board. "What colour do you want to be?" I asked.

"I don't really care," he said, sighing loudly.

It took quite a while to get round the board. In the end I won, but I think by then Grant was giving me easy questions to hurry things up. I mean, are there really questions like "What is the capital of France?"

I put the board away and stood up. "Gee, it sure is getting late," I said, yawning loudly. "No wonder I feel so tired. Doesn't this lake air make you tired?" Grant nodded. "So, I guess I'll see you in the morning then."

"Okay," he said.

"Good night," I said. "Thanks for a very nice day."

"I'll walk you down the hall," he offered.

Our footsteps sounded unnaturally loud on the polished slate of the hallway. When we came to the end I pushed open my bedroom door. "Good night," I said again.

"Don't I even get a good night kiss?" he asked.

I gave him a quick peck on the cheek, then moved back quickly in case he had other ideas. I picked up my pyjamas and my toilet bag and went into the bathroom. After I had finished washing, I cautiously let myself out, peeking into the room to make sure that Grant was not still hovering in the doorway. I let out a sigh of relief that the hallway, as far as I could see it through the partial opening, was clear.

My imagination working overtime again, I thought. *This is Grant, not Joe. Good old boy-scout Grant.*

I slid into the big cold bed, then recoiled violently. Grant was already in it! I scrambled to get back up.

"Don't go, Debbie," he said, holding me in a powerful grip.

"What do you think you're doing?" I demanded, more angry than anything else. "Get out of here right now."

"Come on, Debbie," he said. "I don't think you really want me to go, do you?"

"You better believe I do," I said. "What sort of girl do you think I am?"

He laughed. "Oh, don't play Little Miss Innocent with me," he said. "You've been hanging around all summer with Mr Macho Joe, and I've heard enough about his reputation to know that what he wants, he usually gets."

"Is that why you brought me up here?" I demanded. I could feel my teeth chattering from the cold, but still Grant's grip on me didn't budge one inch. "Because you think I'm easy now?"

"That had something to do with it," he said. "It seemed like the ideal solution."

"To what?"

"To my little problem. I haven't yet … you know … with a girl. I have to before I go up to Harvard."

"Is that part of the admissions procedure?" I demanded.

He gave a sort of half laugh, half cough. "Debbie, I can't go up to Harvard still a virgin," he said. "Everyone would make fun of me. Nobody is a virgin at eighteen these days. You're my last chance."

"Wrong," I said wriggling to get free of him. "Wrong on all counts. First of all, I'm still a virgin, and I intend to stay that way until I meet the right person and it's the right time. Second, I'm not going to be anybody's 'last chance'. I'm surprised at you, Grant. And I want you to let go of me right now."

"Oh, come on, Debbie," he crooned, changing tactics. "You really like me, don't you? This is a terrific chance for both of us. I can understand why you didn't want to with that motorcycle tough, but it will be different with me. I'll be so gentle, Debbie …"

"Don't you understand English, Grant?" I shouted. "No, no, and for the last time no!"

"But Debbie, everybody does it. We're probably the only two oddballs in the whole state. Nobody else makes a big deal about it."

"I don't care what anybody else does or doesn't do," I said. "I just know what I think is right."

But my words didn't seem to have any effect on Grant. He was half crushing me and suddenly I realized that I had no way of fighting him off; he was just too strong. For a second I decided it was hopeless. I had no way of reasoning with Grant, and I had no way of getting out of here. And to think that I had said no to Joe because I wanted to wait, and all I'd waited for is this creep! I sent Joe away when he was the one who really cared about me …

I wasn't struggling anymore, and Grant obviously thought that I'd decided to give up without a fight after all.

"That's right, Debbie," he whispered. "This will be so great."

One of his hands left my wrist to start moving down my body. Without thinking twice I acted. I sank my teeth into his shoulder at the same time as I pushed up on his nose as hard as I could. He let out a cry of pain. Wriggling violently, I finally pulled free. I ran as fast as I could to the front door. Hearing him yell out and start after me, I wrenched the door open and ran. The car and the trees were ghostly shapes in the dark, the driveway a ribbon of white through the darkness.

I glanced over my shoulder to see him running down the path toward me, his body white in the moonlight as he tried to put on a robe and run at the same time.

"Debbie, wait, come back," he was shouting. "I'm sorry. I didn't mean …"

I sprinted as I've never sprinted before, the gravel cutting into my bare feet. Luck was with me there – I walked around barefoot a lot more than Grant, so my feet were tougher. Also I wasn't as heavy. I heard him cursing as the gravel cut into his toes. Ahead of me I could see the wall and the gate. It wasn't fully bolted, thank goodness, or I'd have been trapped. I wriggled through and then slammed the gate shut behind me.

I could hear Grant's voice, yelling out after me. "Debbie, I'm sorry, please come back," he called. "Don't go. Debbie, you can't walk anywhere. It's too far. Don't be an idiot! Please come back!"

I didn't slow down for a minute. I just kept up that half jog, half walk until the sounds of his shouting died in the distance. *I'll walk to that shop,* I thought. *I can call someone from there.*

As my fear ebbed, I became aware of my surroundings. A chilly wind was blowing from the lake, and my little satin pyjamas were no protection against it. My feet were tingling from running over all that gravel, and there was no sign of anything ahead. It hadn't seemed far to the shop by car but what about on foot. Also, what would I do if a car drove past. Would I dare to stop a car full of strangers? Who would I call when I reached the shop? And worst of all, what would I do if Grant came looking for me?

The road dropped down beside the lake. It looked very pretty, shimmering in the moonlight. Another sight looked even prettier: a motorcycle was leaning against a pine tree, and Joe was sitting on a big boulder beside the lake.

Chapter Fifteen

"Joe!" I blurted out, breaking into a run again. "You're still here."

"Oh, hi," he said, not moving from the boulder. "I see you're into midnight jogging. I hear it's very healthy. I like the jogging suit, too – I hear pink satin is very wind resistant. I don't know about the footwear, though. I didn't realize Nike was making invisible running shoes these days. What will they come up with next?"

"I can't believe it. You didn't leave!" I cried, staggering toward him. "I'm so glad to see you."

"Why? You want to push me in the water again?" he asked. "I'd better get off this boulder before you try it." He slid down and began to walk towards his bike.

"Where are you going?" I screamed.

"Home, I guess," he said. "Since you didn't need me anymore, I thought I'd just drive around and enjoy the countryside, but it's getting cold, so I think I'll go home."

"Will you stop teasing for a second!" I shouted.

"Who's teasing?" he asked. "You told me to get out of your life. Fine, you just go where you were going and I'll be on my way."

"Joe, don't do this to me," I said, and burst into tears. "Joe, I need you. I don't care how many times you say 'I told you so,' just don't leave me."

Joe paused, considering. Now that the flood of tears had been unleashed, I couldn't stop shaking. He came over to me. "So you and Mr Perfect didn't get on as well as you thought you would?" he asked.

"Joe, he tried to ... he got into my bed ... he wouldn't stop ... I ... I was so scared!"

He looked at me, obviously realizing what had happened for the first time. In a second his arms were around me. He was stroking the back of my head as if I were a little girl and patting me gently. "There, there, it's okay. It's going to be all right," he whispered.

"Don't leave me," I pleaded.

"Of course I won't leave you."

"Please just keep holding me," I whispered, nuzzling into his shoulder. "You were so right about that creep. I had no idea ... I had no idea that any boy could be like that. He wouldn't let go of me. I kept begging him, but he wouldn't listen ..."

"Damn," Joe muttered almost to himself. "I knew I was right about him. I should never have left you. I'm sorry, Debbie," he said, kissing my hair. "I should have stayed. I should never have let you go in the first place. I did try to warn you."

"I know you did," I said. "I can't think how I could have been so stupid."

"It's not your fault," he said. "You didn't know that not all boys are Mr Nice Guy like me."

"I sure know that now," I said. "You know what really gave me the courage to fight him off? It was thinking that I said no to you when I really meant yes, and there was no way I'd let the first time be with a creep like Grant."

"How did you fight him off?" Joe asked, relief in his voice.

I giggled thinking of it. "I bit him and punched his nose."

I felt him laughing, too. "Hey, not bad! See, I knew spending time with me would teach you a thing or two," he said. "Little gentle Debbie would never have dared do that when I first met her. She'd have been too scared of offending the android."

"You're right," I said, laughing too, through my tears. "I almost did think that."

"Come on," he said, "you're one big shiver. We've got to get you home."

"But I can't ride on a motorcycle in pink pyjamas," I said.

"So we'll go back and pick up your things," Joe said.

"Go back to Grant's?"

Joe chuckled. "I don't think you need to worry if I'm there," he said. "Hold on, I'll just turn the bike round."

He was under the tree wheeling the bike round when headlights lit up the night. Grant's car came round the corner, moving very fast. It screeched to a halt when he saw me, and he leaped out. He didn't even see Joe, who was out of the headlight's beam behind the tree. Grant ran over to me. "Thank heavens, Debbie – there you are," he said. "I was so worried."

"Oh sure," I said. "I noticed at the house how very concerned you were about me. It was touching."

"Look, I've said I was sorry," he said. "I misread the signals back there. It could have happened to anyone. Let's just forget about it, okay? Come on, hop in and I'll drive you back."

"I'm not going anywhere with you, Grant," I said.

"Where else do you think you can go?" he asked, his voice rising in panic. "What will people think if they see you dressed like that? What will your mother say?"

"I expect she'll be really furious," I said, Joe's presence in the darkness giving me warm confidence. "Furious with you, I mean. She always thought you were such a nice boy. Shows how wrong even adults can be, doesn't it?"

"But it was all a mistake," he said, his voice high and pleading now. "I thought that you wanted to come up here with me because . . . look, Debbie, you won't tell your mother, will you? It would get back to my parents—"

"Yes, it would," I said.

"Look, Debbie, be reasonable," he pressed. "Just come back with me. You have nothing to worry about. I'll leave you alone, and I'll drive you home in the morning. We can even go out waterskiing first. Okay?"

"No, it's not okay, Grant," I said. "I'm not going anywhere with you, ever again."

"There's no need to get so hysterical," he said, although he sounded like the one who was getting hysterical. "You're making such a big thing out of nothing."

He came round the car toward me and had almost grabbed my arm when a voice spoke. "You heard her," Joe said, stepping into the light. "She doesn't want to go with you."

To say that Grant was surprised was a massive understatement. His jaw dropped open and he stepped back. "I know you," he said. "You're, er . . ."

"I'm the guy who's girl you've been messing with," Joe said, taking another step towards him, "and I have to tell you, it don't make me very happy."

"But she told me . . ." Grant said, his voice shrill and squeaky now. "She told me it was all over between you. Otherwise I'd never have—" He turned back to me, glaring at me as if I were in the wrong. "I asked you and you said you two were finished."

"So I changed my mind," I said. Now that Joe was standing here beside me, I had an outrageous desire to start giggling. I suppose it was delayed shock.

Grant turned to Joe. "I don't know what she told you, but it isn't true," he said hastily. He sounded really scared. I was used to Joe in his motorcycle outfit, but I guess to a stranger, alone on a very dark road, Joe in his leather jacket did come across as menacing. In fact, Grant started deflating like a balloon with a hole in it in front of my eyes. "As I said to her," he went on, still babbling, "It was all a misunderstanding. I misread the situation back there. I thought she was inviting me into her room. I never dreamed ... I mean, I never would have ... what would you have thought if a girl wanted to come to a cabin alone with you?"

"Only because I thought your parents would be here and you said you just wanted someone to come along for the drive," I blurted out. I turned to Joe because the wind off the water made me start shivering again. "Can we go home now, please?" I asked.

"So you're really going back with him?" Grant asked.

"You don't think I'd want to stay here with you?" I asked incredulously.

Grant looked from me to Joe and back again. "I just don't get it," he said. "You could have had me and you choose him? I don't think much of your taste. In fact, I don't know why I decided to bring you here in the first place. You just don't belong in our group anymore. You fit in better with those condos and the weirdos at that cafe!" He started to walk back to his car. "Enjoy your ride home. Just don't be surprised if Mr Hell's Angel here doesn't want to stop off along the way. Then maybe you'll decide that you'd have been better off with a civilized guy like me!"

Joe walked calmly toward Grant. "Doesn't sound to me like you know what the word *civilized* means," he said.

"I'm sure it's not in your vocabulary," Grant drawled back as they faced each other, almost nose to nose. "After all, it's got more than four letters in it."

"At least I know enough not to mix up *civilized* with *slimy,"* Joe said. I wanted to clap but I kept silent, fascinated, more than anything, by the spectacle of two guys fighting over me.

Grant tried to come up with a good parting shot but obviously couldn't. His brain never did work as fast as Joe's. Instead he started to turn toward his car again. "If I were you," he said, "I'd get back to that greasy spoon where you both belong."

"With pleasure," Joe said. "Let's go get your stuff and then we'll head for home."

A few minutes later I was riding behind Joe over a mountain pass. The moonlight cast stripes of light across the road. The wind was blowing in my face, and I snuggled in close to Joe's big jacket. But somehow, I wasn't even all that cold anymore. I buried my nose in the leather of Joe's jacket, feeling the smooth texture against my cheek. This was a guy who was prepared to take risks for me, to fight for me. I couldn't ask for much more, could I?

At the top of the pass Joe pulled over to the observation area. "Mind if we just admire the view a minute," he said. "I wasn't thinking about views when I came here."

Below us we could see the lake, outlined in silver, the dark shapes of distant peaks, and the moon, floating above the water. The scent of pines was all around us. Joe and I stood beside the rough stone wall, very close but not touching. I felt that I had to say something.

"Joe," I began, "I just want to thank you for everything. You were terrific back there. You showed who really had class."

"Yeah," he said, with some satisfaction. "Just because some guy drives a fancy car and plays a lot of tennis doesn't make him a gentleman, does it?"

"I know that now," I said. A long pause. The wind sighed through the pine branches. Somewhere below a bird called. "I said a lot of awful things, Joe," I began hesitantly. "I thought you'd let me down, and I was hurt and angry. I thought that hurting you back would make me feel better."

"And did it?"

I shook my head. "Worse."

"You certainly know how to hurt a guy," he said at last. "All those punches below the belt."

"I know," I said. "I'm sorry."

"You know what hurt most of all?" he asked. "The fact that you couldn't or wouldn't understand why I sold the cafe. It really hurt me that you thought I'd just go for the money. I thought you knew me better than that."

"I thought I did, too," I said. "It just didn't seem as though there could be any other reason to betray your friends."

"I had two reasons," he said. "The first was Poppa. I knew he'd never retire while the cafe was around. He'd just go on working with his bad heart until he dropped dead beside the french fryer one day. He deserves a peaceful retirement. He's worked hard all his life! Then those hotel guys told me the kind of money they'd be prepared to offer . . . well, it seemed like the answer."

"And the other reason?" I asked, already feeling ashamed of how I had jumped to conclusions."

"The other reason was you," he said.

"Me? What did I have to do with it?" I asked.

"Remember what you said about the Heartbreak not being worth a hill of beans compared to an education? I thought that if the Heartbreak got torn down, my family couldn't lay any more guilt trips on me to work for them anymore. I could really go to college – not just a couple of Mickey Mouse courses to make me feel that I was studying, but a real course load, leading to a real degree. It all seemed so possible. I was sure you'd understand."

I stared down at the silvery lake, feeling the rough coldness of the wall beneath my fingers. Of course I should have understood. He'd tried to tell me, I realized now. He'd tried to explain several times and I – full of my usual self-righteousness – had not wanted to listen.

"Sometimes," I said softly, "I guess I can be a bit pigheaded."

He laughed. "You can say that again."

"The problem is, I always think I'm doing the right thing," I went on. "Everything seems so clear to me at the time. I could see Ashley and Howard and all the rest of the gang with nowhere to go, no cafe they could afford down at the beach, and that seemed terrible. It still does, but I do see your point now, too. You were right to be worried about your grandfather, and you do have a right to go to college. Life just gets more and more complicated."

"So what do we do now?" Joe asked. "I must admit, I didn't think of what would happen to the kids at the cafe until you reminded me. Then I felt bad about it, but it was too late."

"Nothing's final until the environmental impact study is finished, is it?" I asked. "Maybe there's still a way out of selling the cafe – if that's what you want, that is."

"I really want to go to college," he said.

"And you should," I said. "But maybe you can do both."

We stood there looking at each other.

"Did you mean what you said back there?" he asked.

"About what?"

"It sounded like you'd changed your mind about you and me."

"I never really wanted us to break up in the first place," I said quietly. "I just wanted everything to stay the way it was."

Joe put his hands squarely on my shoulders. "Like I told you before, whatever happens to the Heartbreak shouldn't change the way we feel about each other."

"You're right," I said.

"I really care about you," he said quietly. "It hurt me a lot when you shut me out of your life."

"I know you care about me," I said. "You came up here after me . . . you didn't give up on me. That showed me how much you care more than anything else ever could."

He smiled, clearly knowing just how wonderful he had been. "It was driving me crazy, thinking that you might hitch up with that android again!" he said.

"Oh, I see," I said, pulling away from him. "It wasn't my welfare that brought you up here at all. It was your dumb macho jealousy."

"You know what?" Joe asked, looking down at me with amusement in his eyes.

"No, what?"

"You still talk too much," he said, and then kissed me, long and tenderly.

"Oh, Joe," I murmured when he released me again. "I've missed you so much."

"You're right," he said. "Life without the greatest lips in Rockley – no make that in the state – can't have been too much fun!"

"One of these days, Joe Garbarini," I said, lunging at him as he tried to fight me off, "I'm going to show you who's boss!"

"Hey, watch the bike," he called, catching hold of my wrists before I could smash into his motorcycle. "Will you cool it? I don't know … a week without me and I have to start taming you all over again!"

"You taming me? That's a switch. Who's got the biggest ego in Rockley?"

"And who thinks she always knows best?"

"You know what?" I said, not struggling now but gazing up at him with a little smile. "I think we make a great couple, don't you?"

"The greatest," he said, and kissed me gently on the tip of my nose. I slid my arms around his neck and brought my lips toward his to demonstrate what a truly great couple we made!

Chapter Sixteen

I spent the day after my nightmare with Grant recuperating at home. I tried not to say more than I had to to my mother. After letting myself in early in the morning, I faced Mom at breakfast. I told her Grant and I had had a fight, which was true enough. She took it to mean what I had hoped she would and looked disappointed.

"I thought you two would get along so well," she said. "You have so much in common."

"He's so opinionated," I said. "He always wants everything his own way!" Which was also true enough!

She pushed back her hair and sighed. "Oh, well, I suppose parents can't choose their daughters' boyfriends for them," she said.

I grinned. "Your parents didn't like Daddy," I reminded her, "but that didn't stop you."

"Maybe I should have listened to them," she said wistfully.

"But then there wouldn't have been any me," I reminded her.

She laughed and ruffled my hair. "Think of all the worry that would have saved me," she said, and drained the rest of her coffee. The interrogation was thus over painlessly, and I went back to bed for the rest of the morning.

Now that everything was just fine again between Joe and

me, the main problem in life was definitely what to do about the Heartbreak. Men in hard hats were constantly strolling around the cottages behind the cafe, sticking stakes in the ground and measuring things. And the bulldozer was still parked in our car park. You could tell the driver only needed a brief go-ahead nod and he'd wipe out the cafe and everything around it in seconds. Joe was still caught in the middle – not wanting to have the Heartbreak torn down, but also not wanting to run it. I could see now what a hard decision it was for him, and I tried to let him make up his own mind about what was most important to him. If we weren't too late to stop the sale, that was.

Joe and I talked about it over the phone that evening. I let him do most of the talking, batting about the pros and cons of keeping the cafe, but he still couldn't get any nearer to a decision.

"It's my grandfather, Deb," he said. "He's the one I worry about. I mean, if I don't get to college for a couple of years, so what? I can always catch up on my education. But he's seventy-five years old and he's had a major heart attack. He deserves to retire, and he won't do it as long as this cafe is around."

"That's true," I agreed, "but I'm sure you could find a manager for the cafe if you really wanted to – someone who could run the place and free both you and your grandfather to do what you want. Anyway," I added, "we might be discussing all this for nothing. After all, you've signed a contract. I can't see those developers letting you just back out of it."

But at the Heartbreak the next morning, even Joe was able to make up his mind about what to do. When I arrived at work, his grandfather was also there.

"What's he doing here?" I whispered to Joe as soon as Mr Garbarini was out of earshot.

Joe made a face. "Supposed to be doing inventory," he said, "but he's really just here to drive me crazy. He just told me I don't know how to cook hamburgers!"

"In that case, you can do all the cooking this morning,"

I said. "You know what I'm like when I'm nervous. The hamburgers won't stay on the grill and I might just toss one out of the window."

"I thought it was my presence that had that effect on you," Joe said, coming so close to me that we were almost touching.

"Your presence? Nah, I don't feel a thing," I lied.

"Not even if I put my arms round you, like this?" Joe asked, looking down at me in a way that made me melt all the way to my toes, "and then kiss you, like—"

"Mama Mia! Not Again!" Mr Garbarini's voice roared through from the open doorway. "What you think I run here, eh? A nice cafe or an X-rated movie house!"

He came into the kitchen, his spiky white eyebrows dancing up and down as he glared at us. "I stay away from my cafe for a few months and look what happens!" he roared. "No work gets done, always smoochie-smoochie!"

"It's her fault," Joe said quickly. "She leads me astray."

"Hah! Don't believe a word he says, Mr Garbarini! He's the world's biggest con artist," I said.

Mr Garbarini held up his hands, as if praying to heaven for deliverance from young people. "I don't care who's fault it is," he said. "You're both guilty! Now shut up and get back to work! I got customers arriving any minute. You let this place go to pieces while I'm not here. Some grandson I got. Not worth a stick of spaghetti!"

Joe and I grinned at each other.

"One good thing about the cafe closing," Joe said, just loud enough for his grandfather to hear, "Is that we'll have Poppa off our backs. Won't that be great?"

"Cafe closing, cafe closing – don't talk to me about the cafe closing. I heard enough." Mr Garbarini stormed. "All yesterday I got that fat fool from the resort company here following me around. Sign this paper, sign that paper. You going to be happy with this Mr Garbarini. We're really looking out for you, Mr Garbarini. Hah! Crooks. Every one of them, crooks. I don't know why you ever talked me into selling them my cafe."

"Because you're going to have a lot of money to retire on," Joe snapped back.

"Retire? What do I want to retire for? What will I do with myself all day, eh?" Mr Garbarini roared.

"You'll play checkers with your friends at the senior center. You'll play bocce ball with Giovanni and Franco at the park. Enjoy yourself, Poppa, that's what you'll do," Joe said. "Maybe you can even travel to Italy and see all your old relatives."

Mr Garbarini waved his hands up and down. "Why would I want to do dumb stuff like that?" he asked. "Giovanni, he cheat at bocce ball. I see him always kick my ball out of the way. And every time I go to that senior center, old women try to grab me for their husband. And Italy? Italy's full of McDonalds these days. They don't even make a decent red wine there anymore."

"So what do you want to do, Mr Garbarini?" I asked.

He thumped his fist down on the counter so violently that

the dishes all clinked and jiggled. "What do I want to do? Go on working, that's what I want. I want they should carry me out of here in a box when I die – with my spatula still in my hand."

"But Poppa, you should take it easy. You deserve a break," Joe said. "Besides, the doctors keep telling you to rest more."

"Doctors, what do they know?" Mr Garbarini sneered. "They should know that a man is his work. Take away his work and he's nothing. Then is the time to curl up and die."

"So why did you agree to sell the Heartbreak?" I asked cautiously, waiting to be yelled at.

He shrugged his shoulders. "This grandson of mine. He say to me, 'It's a great opportunity, Poppa. They offer so much money, Poppa,' and I think maybe, Okay. Take the fools' money. But now I think, what do I want money for? Now I got to go to the trouble of finding a new cafe to buy, getting it all set up the way I want it." He stroked his nose thoughtfully. "Maybe that's not such a bad thing. This time I get the cafe I want – much bigger than this. With all that money we start over real good, eh, Joe? All chrome and modern, eh? Three or four french fryers. Maybe we get a pizza oven, too. What do you think, Joe?"

Joe had gone very pale. He was staring at his grandfather. "You want to buy a new cafe?" he asked.

"Sure I do."

"Then let's just hope this sale goes through," Joe said. "From what I hear, environmental impact reports are tricky things. They often stop building permits dead in their tracks."

"Mr Grossman said there would be no problem," Mr Garbarini said. "He said nobody's going to make no fuss about the environment in a place like this. They like progress here."

"He's going to be surprised," Joe said. "There are a lot more environmentalists around here than he thinks. In fact, I wouldn't be at all surprised to discover that there is a very good reason why they can't put in this new hotel after all."

As soon as his grandfather left the kitchen, Joe grabbed me. "Quick, you're supposed to be the one with the brains. Start thinking!"

"Of what?"

"Of a way to make sure the environmental impact report says they can't build the resort here!" Joe said.

"I'm flattered by your confidence in me," I said, "but I don't know a thing about the ecology of this area. I know a seal from a seagull and that's about all."

"Then learn," Joe said. "Go and study it at the library or something. We might still be in time to keep the Heartbreak."

"I'll do my best," I said, doubtfully.

I put in a long morning in the reference section the next day, but I didn't really know what I was looking for and I couldn't come up with anything more imaginative than oil slicks. And even I had to admit that it was unlikely a hotel would make an oil slick, unless they overdressed their salads. So I was feeling pretty subdued when I came into the Heartbreak for work. After all, Joe was counting on me to work a miracle and I had failed to produce one.

A group of kids had already gathered at the back table when I came in. Howard was there and so was Art and a whole bunch of surfers. They weren't on the beach because the waves had been too rough ever since the night Joe rescued me. The choppy water was caused, so we heard, by Hurricane Donna, which was sitting off the coast of Mexico, far to the south of us. This had meant no surfing, and in the meantime the cafe had been full of surfers waiting for the red flags to be removed. Ashley was also back and had even brought Jason with her. Now that was progress! They all looked up hopefully as I sat down.

"Found anything?" Joe asked.

"About what?" Art demanded.

"She's been researching ways to stop the development," Joe said. "She knows all about libraries and that stuff."

"There was nothing in the library," I said. "I guess there is nothing of ecological value in this area. We'll have to try a new approach."

"I've got it," Howard said, his Adam's apple bobbing excitedly. "I'll build a giant sea monster and make it cruise up and down the coast!"

"No, Howard," Joe said.

"Or why don't I invent some sort of green slime that clings to things and—"

"No, Howard," Joe said again.

"So what were you looking for?" Jason asked cautiously.

"I don't know," I said. "Maybe some sort of rare animal or bird or something."

"Jason saw a rare bird, didn't you?" Ashley asked, looking up at him adoringly. "It was very pretty. It had these black feathers – like a little black hat. Some sort of pigeon, wasn't it?"

Jason sighed patiently. "It was a crested auklet," he said. "At least. I'm pretty sure it was. I could almost swear it was, although I've never seen one except in a bird book before. They don't usually nest here."

"Jason knows a lot about birds," Ashley said proudly. "He said this one had never been seen before in this area."

Jason's face was slightly pink. "Birds are actually my hobby," he said.

"And you think you've found something rare here?" Joe asked.

Jason's face became even pinker as everyone looked at him. "It's, uh, possible that it was just here by accident, blown in by a gale, maybe. Or maybe I could have made a mistake, although I don't think so."

"I'm sure you didn't," Ashley said loyally. "We looked it up in that bird book in the bookshop."

"So where did you see it?" Joe asked impatiently.

"It appeared to be nesting in the cliffs."

"Nesting in the cliffs?" Joe said, beaming at me.

"And all that construction noise would certainly startle it," I added.

"Definitely. It would probably never be seen in this area again!" We grabbed each other and danced around excitedly while the others looked on, not sure whether we hadn't finally flipped.

"Would someone mind telling me what's going on – in plain English?" Art said at last. "Has the whole world taken up bird-watching or something?"

"Don't you get it?" Joe said, still clutching my shoulders excitedly. "If a rare bird is nesting here for the first time, they won't allow construction of the hotel here!"

"We might be able to save the Heartbreak after all!" I added.

"I thought you were the one who wanted to sell it?" Art said, looking confused.

"Only because he wanted his grandfather to retire," I explained. "But his grandfather has said he won't retire anyway. He'd just buy another cafe instead."

"Oh," Art said, still trying to get things straight.

"Ashley, I'm so glad you brought Jason here," I said. "We're lucky he knows about birds and things."

"It was fate," Ashley said. "We're ruled by fate, you know. Besides, he's a Taurus and I'm a Capricorn. It was destined in the stars."

Joe looked at me and winked. "I guess a new paper has just come out at the supermarket," he said.

"It's no joke," Ashley said, looking hurt. "The stars really do control our lives."

"So what about Debbie and me?" Joe asked. "What sign are you, Deb?"

"Libra."

"And I'm an Aries. Are we supposed to get along?"

"No! You're absolute opposites," Ashley said. "Debbie should date another air sign, not fire."

"You know Debbie, she likes playing with fire. Don't you, Deb?" he asked, giving me a wink.

"I do not," I said haughtily. "I'd prefer a peaceful, quiet life, only I'm stuck with you guys and because of that, life is never peaceful or quiet."

"Speaking of not being peaceful," one of the guys chimed in, "did you hear the news this morning that Hurricane Donna is moving up the coast?"

"They don't think it will come this far north, do they?" I asked.

"Hey, that would be neat," Art exclaimed. "Imagine surfing on 40-foot waves!"

"If there were 40-foot waves, this whole town would be underwater," Howard commented.

"Great, I could ride my board right to the door of the Heartbreak," Art said, and all his buddies laughed.

We all joked about it that afternoon, as if hurricanes and other disasters were something that only happened to other people.

Chapter Seventeen

The next day nobody was joking anymore. The TV news had shown Hurricane Donna, a big swirl of white clouds moving up the coast, gathering strength and speed. At first Mom and I watched the news pictures of lashing rains and bending palm trees as news stories only, then we began to pay more attention, and finally our local news stations ran interviews with weather experts and explanations on when hurricane watches became hurricane warnings.

"I'd rather you didn't go down to the cafe," my mother said. "I feel uneasy with you down at the beach."

"Well, I feel uneasy with you cruising around getting news stories, so we're even," I said, then relented. "Don't worry, Mom. I don't want to watch the forty-foot waves like some of the kids. Besides, they still don't know where it will come ashore. It could blow right past us."

"Let's hope it does," my mother said, "although everyone down at the paper is itching for a good disaster story."

When I got down to the Heartbreak, it seemed that all the kids there were also itching for the excitement of a real hurricane.

"Imagine watching all those boutiques on Beach Row go

floating away and ending up in Alaska or someplace," someone joked. "Do you think they'll be able to sell their bikinis to the Eskimos?"

"I wonder why they didn't call it Hurricane Debbie?" Joe put in. "That would have been a much better name!"

They went on joking until the police finally showed up at the cafe advising us to leave. "Don't stay here too long or you might find the roads away from the beach jammed," the officer said. "Donna might come ashore late this afternoon, and if she does, this beachfront area will be very badly hit.

Some kids left right away, while others were determined to stay on and see for themselves.

"I wonder if it will be like the disaster movies," Howard asked, his eyes sparkling with excitement, "You know, people clinging to collapsing buildings, getting swept away … aahhh!" This made a few more kids hurry out, and now only the three of us and Art and a few surfers were left.

By this time the wind was already buffeting the cafe, and hail peppered the windows. The sky was very dark.

"I think we ought to go, Joe," I whispered to him. "No sense in staying around any longer."

Joe nodded. "Yeah, we should get these guys out of here safely. I don't want them hanging around and getting swept off by giant waves." He clapped his hands above the noise of the storm. "Okay, we're about ready to close up. Seems like the storm's about to hit, and we don't want to get caught down here. If you guys can help us bring everything inside, we'll close up and get out of here."

Outside it was hard to stand up straight. We heard garbage

can lids go clanking by as we brought our own cans inside and locked the back door.

"Maybe it will blow the bulldozer away," one of the guys joked.

"Yeah, it'd serve them right."

A tile came flying off our roof. Debris from the old fishermen's cottages was being flung around. The sky out at sea was almost black. A police car was cruising Beach Row, its loudspeaker telling people to get out. Joe grabbed me as an umbrella came sailing past. It was green and white and had La Lanterna written all over it. It came to rest against our back fence.

"We should take this back to them and complain that it nearly hit us and they should watch where they leave their property," Joe said with a grin.

"They're in big trouble if they haven't taken all that outdoor stuff in by now," I said. "Maybe we should go and see if they need help."

"Help those creeps?" Art demanded. "They'd be real happy if the Heartbreak got blown away."

"That doesn't mean we should behave like jerks too," Joe said. "Come on, let's get the umbrella back to them."

We staggered back with it, fighting the force of the wind and the stinging rain. As we came round the corner, we found Beach Row in a state of total chaos. It really did look like one of Howard's disaster movies: people were running up and down, mindlessly waving their arms and screaming, fighting to hold down flying tablecloths and get awnings rolled up. It was clear that they had left everything until too late and now there were too few people to get the job done. We didn't even wait to ask if they needed us – we just plunged right in, dragging tables inside the cafes, helping tape over the bigger windows, rescuing tubs of flowers. As we worked, we could hear the storm outside growing in intensity. Before it had sounded like any old storm – now it sounded like ten storms rolled into one. The wind screamed and howled so loudly that we couldn't shout above it. Rain lashed at the windows and the surf thundered so close that we expected the next wave to come crashing through the walls. Until now I had been worried, but not really scared. In a way it was exciting to face a hurricane. It would be the sort of thing we could tell friends about later: "Yeah, we stayed down at the beach and watched the hurricane come in. It was no big deal."

But suddenly I wanted to get out of there. I remembered how the kids had joked about Beach Row floating off to Alaska, and it no longer seemed either ridiculous or funny. I didn't want to be trapped in one of those boutiques when the waves finally broke over the wall. I glanced at the guys. They were still having a great time, working like crazy but joking as they passed each other. I tried to swallow back my fear because, obviously, I couldn't leave without Joe. I was really glad to see the police car again and to hear it ordering: "Leave everything and go right now." They didn't need to tell me twice!

Almost as they said it a wave broke over the sea wall and water rushed down Beach Row. The boutique owners scrambled for their cars, and our kids ran back to the cafe. It was easy to run because the wind pushed at our backs, making us feel almost as if we were flying. The horrible fear rose inside me that if I stumbled, the wind would snatch me up like a kite. Joe must have sensed my fear because he reached out and grabbed me, holding me firmly next to him. The next wave caught us, almost sweeping us off our feet even though we were well back from the ocean by now. Pieces of roof were peeling off several cottages.

We reached the Heartbreak. "Get in my car," I shouted to Joe.

"Are you crazy?" he yelled back. "I can't leave my bike here!"

"You can't ride a bike in this! You'll be blown over if you even try!"

"I'm not going to leave it here to get salt water in it!"

"Joe! You can't ride a bike. Get in the car!" I grabbed at his arm.

He shook me off. "You go if you want," he said. "I'll wheel it round to the back porch. At least it won't get blown over there."

He walked calmly over to his bike and began wheeling it, fighting to keep the heavy motorcycle upright against the force of the wind. I stood beside my car, holding onto it for security, not knowing what to do. My fear for Joe was as great as my fear for myself. Part of me longed to drive up that hill to safety, but the other part knew full well that I could not leave Joe down at the beach. I longed to grab him and force him into my car, but he had his mouth set in a determined line, and I knew that it was going to take more force than I had to pry him loose from his precious bike! At last I couldn't bear to watch him struggling any longer. I let go of the car and struggled over to join him.

The moment I let go, a huge gust of wind, stronger than any of the ones before it, caught me, sending me sprawling to my knees. I crouched down, too terrified to move as branches and boards sailed past me. Then there was a creaking, groaning sound right beside me and I watched the roof of the Heartbreak porch lift off and go flying toward Joe. It all seemed to happen in slow motion, like the scene from *The Wizard of Oz* when the house falls out of the sky. The porch roof really was spinning crazily, lifted by updrafts before it came spiraling down right where Joe and the bike were.

Joe had his back to it. I tried to yell above the noise, but even my loudest scream didn't carry that far. So I sprinted toward him and flung myself at him, making him let go of the bike and stumble backward. We both fell heavily onto the mud and the porch roof crashed to the ground beside us. Sea water came rushing up the street, swirling icy cold around us. I couldn't tell if I had reached Joe before the roof struck him or not. He was lying very still.

"Joe!" I yelled, patting his face. "Joe, speak to me!"

Slowly his eyes opened and focused on me. He grinned. "See, I told you you were crazy about me," he said. "You can't even keep your hands off me in the middle of a hurricane. But I don't mind," he said, wrapping his arms around me to trap me close to him. "Nobody's watching, are they?"

"You crazy idiot," I shouted, laughing with relief as I pushed his lips away from me. "We're about to be swept away by giant waves."

"I thought it felt cold and wet," Joe said, sitting up slowly. "So would you mind telling me what this was all about? One minute I'm wheeling my bike, the next I'm tackled and half knocked out by a crazy woman."

"I had to get you out of the way in a hurry. That was about to fall on you," I said, indicating the large piece of roof, tiles still intact, that was lying inches from his left hand. It now almost covered his bike. Just the front wheel stuck out.

Joe scrambled to his feet. "My bike!" he cried. He tried to lift the roof. "My God, this thing weighs a ton," he said, and turned back to me, white faced as he realized how close he'd come to disaster. "You just saved my life," he said. "If this had hit me, I'd be dead!"

We stood there, gazing at each other while the rain and wind swept around us. He held out his hands to me. "You're terrific, you know that," he said gently.

"You're not so bad yourself."

"You saved my life."

"So? You rescued me from Grant."

"I guess that makes us even."

"I guess it does," I said. We grinned at each other with new-found closeness. Then a realization dawned on me. "No more of this male superiority nonsense, okay?" I shouted, putting my hands up to his cold cheeks, "because if I hear any more of your chauvinist ideas, I'll tell the world I rescued you from a hurricane."

"You want me to tell the world what I rescued you from?" he asked.

"On second thought, maybe not," I said. He kissed me gently, his cold lips touching mine.

"So I guess that means we just have to keep our secret to ourselves," he said. "Come on, let's get out of here."

"What about your bike?"

He looked back at it, then back at me. "There's no way we can lift that roof, and besides, it's insured. I'd rather get you home safely," he said. "I can always get another bike. I don't think there are too many Debbie Lesleys floating around though."

I grinned as he helped me into the car and started up the engine.

"Thank heavens," he added.

"That the car started?"

"That there aren't more Debbie Lesley's around. One is all I can handle," he said, and put his foot on the gas as we roared up the canyon.

Chapter Eighteen

When we pulled up outside the condo, my mother's car wasn't in the garage.

"I hope she's safe," I said, looking around anxiously. Up here the force of the storm was not so terrible, but the ground was littered with tree branches and dustbin lids, and it was still raining like crazy.

"You want me to come in and wait with you until she gets back?" Joe asked.

I nodded. "Unless you really want to get home first," I said.

"I'll call my folks from here," he said. "They'll want to know what's happening down at the cafe."

We let ourselves in to the empty apartment. It felt cold and drafty inside. I couldn't stop shivering. I looked over at Joe and saw he was shivering, too.

"We look like a couple of drowned rats," I said, laughing uneasily.

"That's what happens when you lie around in freezing sea water," Joe said.

"Do you want to take a shower?" I asked.

"After you, madam," he said with a mock bow. "Anyway, I should phone my folks first."

I went into my room and came out with a big towel.

"Here, wrap this around yourself," I said. "I'll put a kettle on for tea."

I didn't let myself linger too long in the blissfully hot water, remembering that our puny little water heater wouldn't heat enough water for two showers if I was greedy. After drying off, I put on a tracksuit, wrapped my head in a towel, and came out just as the kettle was starting to boil. Joe was standing awkwardly in the kitchen, trying to work out which cabinet we kept the tea in.

"You go and shower," I said. "I'll make the tea."

I'd just finished making the tea and was sipping a cup, breathing in the comforting steam, when the front door opened with a bang and my mother came rushing in.

"Thank God," she panted. "I've never been so relieved to see your car in my life."

"I've been home for a while," I said. "We left when the police made us get out."

"I know," she said, still panting. "I couldn't stand it any longer at the newspaper. We got all these reports about Rockley Beach being flooded and damaged. Finally, I just left. I drove straight to Rockley and found the road closed. I hoped you'd got out safely, but there was nobody around to ask. My imagination worked overtime all the way home."

"You worry too much," I said, handing her a cup of tea. "You have a very sensible daughter, you know. I could tell it was time to get out, mostly because of the giant waves sweeping up the street!"

She took the tea. "I keep forgetting you're not a little girl anymore who has to be looked after," she said. "Once a mother, always a mother, I suppose. I have to fight the instinct to pick you up from school every day!"

"I'm a big girl now," I said. "You can count on me to behave in a mature fashion from now on. In fact . . ."

The rest of the sentence was drowned out by Joe's voice singing loudly. Before I could say anything more, he emerged from the bathroom with a towel wrapped around his waist, drying his hair with another towel.

"One slight problem we overlooked," he said, not noticing my mother. "I forgot to bring any extra clothes with me."

My mother's face was a picture of horror and embarrassment.

"Mom," I said hastily, "you remember Joe, don't you?."

"Very well," she said.

"Oh, hi, Mrs Lesley," Joe said, not in the least concerned. "I didn't hear you come in."

"So I noticed," she said.

"Joe's bike got crushed under a piece of falling roof, so we had to come here," I said. "We were both soaked because we stayed to help the people on Beach Row get their places boarded up."

My mother looked from Joe to me and nodded.

"I'll put your clothes in the dryer," I said to Joe, "and then I'll find you my extra tracksuit."

"Thanks," he said, following me into the bedroom. I came right out and glared at my mother. "I can tell what you're thinking," I said. "You still don't trust Joe, do you?"

My mother played with the handle of her teacup. "You have to admit, it's not easy for a mother to come home and see a boy wearing only a towel come out of the bathroom," she said.

"No, at least not until her daughter explains that he'd just taken a shower because his clothes were dripping wet and he'd just missed being killed by an inch," I said.

Her face showed the alarm. "You said you got out while it was still safe!"

"We didn't count on a roof landing on us," I said. "It just missed Joe."

"Only because Debbie threw me out of the way and saved my life," he said, coming out of the bedroom looking ridiculous in my pink tracksuit, which barely came down to his knees and elbows. "My colour, don't you think?" he asked, turning around coyly to model for me. I giggled. "You did that, Debbie," Mom asked, her voice shaky.

"I saw the roof coming and he didn't," I said matter-of-factly.

"That was a very brave thing to do," Mom said. "And foolish, too."

"I wasn't going to let a roof land on him like the house landing on the Wicked Witch of the East," I said, laughing uneasily. "Besides, he came to save me earlier."

"When was that?" Mom asked sharply, and I remembered, too late, that she knew nothing about the Grant episode. It just showed how a little sea water could scramble your brains.

"Same sort of thing," I said quickly. "Falling roof!"

I saw Joe stifle a chuckle.

"It sounds really terrible down there," she said. "Thank heavens the road was closed and they wouldn't let us down the canyon or Ralph would have been all for standing amid the flying rooftops and giant waves, interviewing people as they were swept past!"

"I thought newspaper people liked to live dangerously," I said. "You didn't want to get your scoop on the destruction of Rockley at any cost?"

She shuddered and gulped her tea. "Not me," she said. "And if I'd seen my little girl flinging people out of the way of falling roofs, my heart would probably have stopped completely."

I shrugged as if it was no big deal. "It's all over and we're all safe, so let's forget about it, okay?"

I handed Joe a cup. "Here, have some tea. You're still blue," I said.

He took the cup and sipped at it. "What is this?" he asked suspiciously.

"Herb tea – do you like it?"

"It's, um, different," he said.

"I thought we might start selling it at the cafe," I said with a grin.

He made a face. "Over my dead body," he said.

"I could have arranged that a little while ago," I said with a sweet smile. "Drink it. It's supposed to calm your nerves."

"That's it, then," Joe said with a grin. "I don't need it – nerves of steel, that's me."

"I certainly needed it," my mother said, putting down her empty cup. "My nerves have been frazzled all day. Not only from worrying about you, but the way they were all behaving up at the newspaper."

"Hot scoop on the hurricane?" I asked.

She sighed. "Those people are monsters, Debbie," she said. "I went down the coast with Ralph to survey the damage down there. You should have seen it – houses completely flattened or washed away by the waves. And you know what Ralph does? He gets out his little notebook and starts questioning people: 'Was this your house?' 'What will you do now?' No compassion at all. Those people had just lost everything, and he kept on questioning."

"That's Ralph for you," I said, secretly delighted. "The total newspaperman."

"There was this one family," she said slowly. "The father was still missing, and Ralph had to get all the details no matter how upset they got! I was shocked."

"That's his job, Mom," I said. "That's what newspaper people are paid to do."

"I know," she said. "And that's what made me decide that newspaper work is not for me. Tomorrow I'm going to see if it's too late to register at the college for this semester."

"You're going back to college after all?" I exclaimed. "Way to go, Mom!"

"Yeah, way to go, Mrs Lesley," Joe said with enthusiasm. "We might even have some of the same classes!"

We both looked up at him. "You're going to Shoreline?" my mother asked at the same time I did.

He blushed a little. "Yeah, I had a little talk with Poppa. I explained it to him straight that I had to get ahead with my own life. I told him to hire a manager if he opens a new cafe."

"And what did he say?" I asked incredulously, trying to imagine anyone saying anything like that to old Mr Gar-barini and living to tell about it.

Joe shrugged as if it was no big thing. "He understood," he said. "He wants me to get an education – I'd be the first member of our family to go to college! He's boasting about it to his friends already."

"Now you two will be able to talk intellectual college talk over my head," I said, looking lovingly at both of them.

"I don't know if you could really describe Shoreline as intellectual," my mother said hastily. "It's only a community college, after all. I hope Joe won't be disappointed."

"Oh, I don't intend to stay there," Joe said. "I plan to get all those boring old requirements out of the way there and then have saved enough to transfer somewhere more competitive."

My mother was looking more interested and impressed by the minute. "Oh, where do you plan to transfer to, Joe?" she asked.

"Harvard, I thought," Joe said, imitating Grant perfectly. "I think I'm Harvard material."

My mother glared at me, not knowing why I was giggling uncontrollably.

Joe stayed late into the evening, and we talked while my mother made spaghetti and fussed over us. We all talked a lot, about college and our future plans and dreams, and I noticed, by the end of the evening, that my mother wasn't talking to Joe as if he was a refugee from a street gang anymore. She even laughed at his jokes and positively blushed when he told her that she should sign up for the dance class because she still had a great figure!

So one good thing came out of the hurricane, I thought as I drove down to the beach with Joe early the next morning to survey the damage. I could never have guessed what other good things had come from it too.

Rockley Beach was a sorry sight as we pulled off the canyon road. Seaweed, driftwood, and all kinds of other debris littered the pavement way above the Heartbreak, showing just how far the waves had come. Luckily the Heartbreak, built up on pilings as all the old buildings were, had survived with just the damage to its porch roof. The buildings down on Beach Row had not been as lucky. La Lanterna's deck was buried under sand, and one wall looked as if an elephant had leaned against it. Waves had battered the backs of all the buildings, smashing windows and demolishing storage rooms. Their owners were walking around with dazed expressions on their faces, picking up damaged merchandise or sweeping out sand and water. The one good thing was that, thanks to our help in boarding up the front windows, no glass had been broken and no water had come in through shopfronts.

We were just turning back to the Heartbreak when Mr Garbarini emerged from his car. He took in the scene with one sweeping glance.

"Any damage to the cafe?" he asked Joe.

"Only the porch," Joe said.

"Electricity on?" he asked.

Joe nodded.

"Gas still working?"

Joe nodded again.

"Then what are you both waiting for?" Mr Garbarini thundered. "We're the only place with power – and all these folks have got to eat somewhere. For once La Lanterna has to come to us! Get that coffee going! I'm phoning your dad to bring down some doughnuts. We'll make a fortune with all the workmen they'll need to get back in business, plus all the crazy sightseers, too!"

With Joe's grandfather barking orders, Joe and I worked nonstop, making platter after platter of french fries, pot after pot of coffee. One by one the cafe kids trickled in. You could see the relief on their faces when they saw the cafe in full operation. Ashley came in alone around midday and beamed at me.

"No Jason today?" I asked.

She shook her head. "He has to stay at home and help clean up. A tree came down outside his house."

"Really?" I asked. "I wouldn't have thought the winds were that strong all the way up at the country club."

Her face flushed with colour. "He, er, doesn't actually live up at the country club," she said. "He lives just up the coast at Bayside Estates."

"That's where Pam lives," I said in surprise. "The houses there are very ordinary."

She nodded. "I got it all wrong," she whispered. "The BMW belonged to his friend's mother. He was driving it the night we met and I assumed it was his, so he had to keep on borrowing it because he thought I was from the country club and he didn't want to admit he came from Bayside. Isn't that a riot?"

I grinned. "So who confessed first?" I asked.

"He did," she said. "He called his home yesterday and found that a tree had come down and he had to rush back. I said I'd come with him and that's when it all came out."

"Oh Ashley," I said. "All that time you spent deceiving each other."

"Only because we didn't want to lose each other," she said.

"Thank heaven it all turned out all right in the end," I said.

"Yes, especially since Jason's rare bird is going to save the cafe for us," she said.

"I wonder," I said, staring out of the window at the flattened fences and drifting sand. "I wonder if this hurricane will make any difference as far as the development goes?"

"It already did half the work for them by blowing down most of Rockley Beach," Joe commented dryly. "They probably engineered it."

"How could they?" I asked, laughing.

"You know big business," he said. "I bet they have a hot line to heaven!"

I laughed, then I grabbed Joe's arm. "Look, isn't that the owner of La Lantema coming over here? And that's the little guy from Secret Hangups."

"Probably finally decided to see what good food tastes like," Joe said, following their progress across our car park.

"Quick, what can we serve them?" I asked. "Should I run out and get some croissants?"

"We'll serve what we always serve," Joe said. "It's either burgers and fries or starve."

The two men came in cautiously, looking around as if they had never seen a place like this before.

"Hey, it's quite cosy in here," one of them said.

"Can I help you?" I asked.

"Is the owner here?" the man from La Lantema asked.

"Mr Garbarini or his grandson?" I said. "They're both here right now."

"Both of them, then."

I went and got them. Joe looked suspicious. "They've got a nerve," he said to his grandfather. "I wouldn't have thought they were in a position to make any demands right now."

Both Garbarinis walked out of the kitchen. I was struck by how alike they were, walking with something of a swagger, both muscular and powerful. I couldn't help thinking that if I were little Mr Secret Hangups, I'd turn and run.

When Mr Garbarini roared. "Whatta you want?" I actually did see Mr Secret Hangups look at the door.

"We've come on behalf of the Beach Row Association," the owner of La Lanterna began.

"Yeah?" Mr Garbarini demanded.

"We just wanted to say, er, we held an emergency meeting this morning—"

"Yeah?"

"And . . . we feel that the young people from the cafe . . . well, we owe them an apology."

"They were wonderful yesterday, positively wonderful," the man from Secret Hangups chimed in.

"They risked their own safety to help us, and because of them the damage is not catastrophic," the restaurant owner said. "No glass broken and most of our merchandise saved."

"It could have been disastrous, positively disastrous," the owner of Secret Hangups chimed in again.

"So we wanted to tell you," the guy from La Lanterna said, glaring at the other man to silence his constant interruptions, "that we are asking the resort people from Paradise Inns to look elsewhere. If they won't, and I rather suspect they might not, then we'll do everything in our power to make sure that environmental impact report comes out against the development."

"That shouldn't be too hard since two of our Beach Row owners are on the town council," the man from Secret Hangups added.

The owner of La Lanterna held out his hand. "We hope the cafe will stay and we can enjoy each other as neighbours for many years to come."

Joe's grandfather thrust out his own hand and the two men shook. "Come and sit down," he said loudly. "I'm going to cook you the best food you've ever had!"

Late that evening, when the cafe had quieted down and only a few customers remained, Joe and I went to stand out on the roofless porch. The storm had completely blown itself out, and the sky out to sea was streaked with delicate shades of pink and gold. Joe slipped an arm round my shoulders. "So we didn't need Jason's bird after all," he said quietly. "Everything worked out just fine."

I nodded. "Who would have thought a hurricane would solve all our problems," I asked.

"I could have told you about hurricanes long ago," Joe said.

I turned to him. "How come?"

"I knew they were special the moment my own little hurricane blew in last April, accusing me of stealing her parking place," he said with a big smile.

"You did not think I'd come to solve all your problems, Joe Garbarini," I said, my eyes challenging his. "You thought I was a snotty little spoilt brat, and when you heard I was going to be working with you, you thought it was the worst news ever."

"That was just on the surface," he said, slipping his arms round my waist. "Deep down inside me, something said, 'Here is the answer to all your problems. Nothing will ever be boring again!'"

I laughed. "That was true enough," I said. "It hasn't been boring, has it? Infuriating sometimes, and funny and sad, but never boring."

"That's the way I like it," he said, gazing down at me tenderly. "That's how I want my life to be – funny, exciting, scary, even sad, but never boring. Promise you'll stick around for a while to make sure things stay that way."

"I might," I said, "if nothing better comes along."

"Like an invitation to the lake, maybe?"

"Actually, I guess I have to keep an eye on you in case there are any more falling roofs," I said, wrapping my arms around his neck and gazing up into those warm brown eyes.

"That's right,"he said. "There might be another hurricane sometime."

We stood there, just smiling into each other's eyes. Slowly we moved towards each other as if drawn by invisible strings until our lips met very gently. Joe let out a sigh of content and drew me close to him, crushing his lips against mine. A delicious warmth and tenderness flooded over me. I didn't even stop to think that we were standing out on a porch, in full view of Rockley Beach. It didn't seem to matter anymore. Nothing mattered anymore except me and Joe and the fact that he wanted me to stick around for a long, long while.

We might have stayed like that all evening, but a huge bellow blasted into our ears. "Mama mia, not again! This is a good cafe, a respectable place!" Joe's grandfather was standing behind us, his eyebrows going up and down, his arms waving dramatically. "Every time my back is turned! The french fries burn! The poor customers starve! Does my grandson care? No, all he cares about is smooching on the front steps."

Joe laughed. "Poppa, calling it smooching went out with poodle skirts," he said.

"Smooching, necking, making out – what do I know? I'm just an old man," Mr Garbarini said. "But I do know that this is my cafe, and I aim to keep on running it for many years to come. And if you and Miss Debbie Lesley want to keep working here, you'll get inside and clean up that kitchen right now!"

Joe took my hand and grinned at me as we walked back towards the kitchen. "Just think," he said, "we could get fired and start working somewhere civilized like La Lanterna."

I shook my head. "Boring," I muttered. "There's nowhere like the Heartbreak, even if the owner is a slavedriver."

"I heard that!" Mr Garbarini boomed.

Giggling, we ran into the kitchen.

Heartbreak Café

1

NO EXPERIENCE REQUIRED

JANET QUIN-HARKIN

It's 1989. Life's easy for DEBORAH LESLEY: she's up-market, drives her own flash car to school, and looks pretty good too. She's never had a job, either; but now her parents have split up, and she needs the money.

JOE GARBARINI is cool. He likes motorbikes, girls, and fun. He doesn't have time for much — he's running Heartbreak Cafe when he's not at school.

The Heartbreak Cafe is a noisy hangout on the north Californian coast. Joe's worked there for years, and knows what it takes. He's sure Debbie won't last a month — but Debbie's determined to put up with his wisecracks and prove him wrong.

Debbie, Joe and the rest of the gang are all at the Heartbreak Cafe. Meet them in this sparkling new series from bestselling author Janet Quin-Harkin.

www.HeartbreakCafe.LA

Heartbreak Café 2

THE MAIN ATTRACTION

JANET QUIN-HARKIN

Deborah Lesley's parents have split up. She and her mother live in a tiny apartment in a second-rate condominium, and Debbie's had to get an after school job as a waitress to earn extra money.

JOE GARBARINI is the manager of the Heartbreak Café — when he's not at school. He's super-cool, Mr Macho himself, and great on a motorbike. He and Debbie just DO NOT get on.

Movie-madness comes to Rockley Beach and the Heartbreak Café. The place is filled with kids trying to sign on as extras, and only Debbie and Joe seem to be unaffected — until Joe is asked to ride stunts on his motorbike, and he goes crazy too.

Debbie and Joe and Ashley and Howard and the rest of the gang are all here again in this second book in the Heartbreak Café series by bestselling author Janet Quin-Harkin.

www.HeartbreakCafe.LA

Heartbreak Café

3

AT YOUR SERVICE

JANET QUIN-HARKIN

Nothing seems to be going right for Debbie Lesley and her first ever job at the Heartbreak Café. She and Joe Garbarini — who runs the place — don't often have a civil word for each other, and to make matters worse, Joe's glamorous girlfriend Wendy takes over Debbie's daytime shift. Then the sparks really fly, and Debbie's desperate. She doesn't know where to turn. Her best friend Pam has taken up with a drag-racing rock singer, her boyfriend Grant is now an ex-boyfriend, and even her mother is going out on dates. What's happening to her life?

Read about Debbie and Joe and the rest of the gang in this third book in the Heartbreak Café series by best-selling author Janet Quin-Harkin.

www.HeartbreakCafe.LA

Heartbreak Café 4

CATCH OF THE DAY

JANET QUIN-HARKIN

It's a busy summer at the Heartbreak Cafe, but Deborah Leslie has got more than her job as a waitress to deal with.

She still doesn't know where she stands with Joe Garbarini — they spend all their time hurling insults at each other across the kitchen — and even her father doesn't seem to need her any more. Then there's her friend Art, a typical Californian surfer, without a care in the world — until he falls for a beautiful Mexican girl he saved from drowning. Only Debbie knows the danger Art is in, but to help him she's going to need Joe's support.

The rest of the gang are also here with Debbie and Joe in this fourth book in the Heartbreak Cafe series by best-selling author Janet Quin-Harkin.

www.HeartbreakCafe.LA

Heartbreak Café

5

LOVE TO GO

JANET QUIN-HARKIN

At last everything is going right for Deborah Lesley— her best friend is working with her at the Heartbreak Cafe, it's a beautiful summer, and now Joe Garbarini, the cool, macho manager, has finally decided that they make a great couple . . .

But Debbie feels instinctively that trouble is on the way when a mysterious girl, dressed in black, appears in the cafe. Maybe she's being paranoid — Joe thinks she's over-reacting again — but Debbie is determined to stick to her principles.

The rest of the gang are all here in this fifth book in the Heartbreak Cafe series by bestselling author Janet Quin-Harkin.

www.HeartbreakCafe.LA

Publisher - Feb 2021

Printed in Great Britain
by Amazon

56490205R00106